PARADISE BARN

- You ca—
  but no—
- Items—
  Please—
  retur—
- Items—
  custo—
- Renew—
  emai—
  card—
- Plea—
  any —

PARADISE BARN

VICTOR WATSON

Catnip

CATNIP BOOKS
Published by Catnip Publishing Ltd
14 Greville Street
London EC1N 8SB

This edition first published 2009
3 5 7 9 10 8 6 4

Text copyright © Victor Watson, 2009
Map copyright © Suzy Durham, 2009
The moral rights of the author and illustrator have been asserted.

A CIP catalogue record for this book is available from the British
Library.

ISBN 978-1-84647-091-2

Printed in Poland

www.catnippublishing.co.uk

for

Judy,

Sally, Lucy, Tim

and

Florence, Lydia, Sophie and Connie

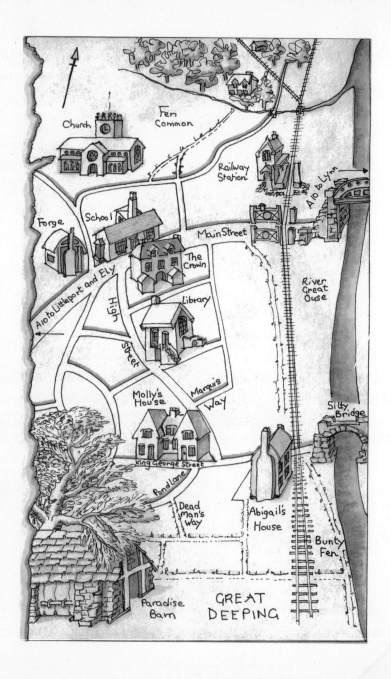

On their way home from school, Molly Barnes and her best friend Abigail took the long way round, then turned into Dead Man's Way. It used to be called *Public Footpath* but Abigail had re-named it.

The path went by a big flat field and ran alongside a dry ditch full of grass and seeding cow-parsley. They held hands as they walked.

There was a row of big elm trees. At the third tree, they stopped. 'That was where his feet were,' Abigail said. She pointed at a patch of grass and nettles, still flattened a little.

'And that was where his head was,' Molly said. She was pointing at the bottom of the elm trunk, about six feet away from where Abigail had been pointing.

'There was dried black blood all over his head,' Abigail whispered.

'And he was wet all over because it had been raining,' Molly said.

'Dead from head to toe!' Abigail added.

Molly knew her friend was trying to give them both the shudders. But it was hard to feel frightened – the sun was shining from an innocent and cloudless sky, one or two of their schoolmates were ahead of them along the path, and Miss Hatch, who taught the little ones, had just gone into her cottage in Pond Lane. Before the War, Miss Hatch used to drive home in her tiny Austin, but now the car stood in its garage with its wheels off, propped on four stacks of bricks. Molly knew because she had seen it there. It would stay like that until the War was over and there would be plenty of petrol again.

Barely one field away stood Paradise Barn, one of their favourite and special places, darkly silhouetted against the bright afternoon sky.

'Only three weeks ago,' Abigail said, 'he walked along this very path and met his doom – right here!'

'Does it scare you?' Molly asked.

'Doesn't it scare *you*?'

Molly thought for a moment. 'No,' she said. 'But I suppose I'd be scared if I met the person who did it.'

'The *murderer*,' said Abigail, '– whoever he was.' For the killer had not been found. The police had been enquiring, but it was Wartime and – like everyone else – they had too much to do. So far, they hadn't even discovered who the dead man was.

Old Miss Morton had found the body. She had been walking her two labradors. Now, whenever Molly saw Miss Morton, she looked carefully at her, imagining there would be a new and special grimness on her face because she had found a dead body. But Miss Morton had always looked grim, even before she had come across the man lying under the elm tree with a bullet-wound in his head.

'What worries you most in the whole world?' Abigail asked.

Molly began to feel careful. She knew what worried Abigail most. Nobody knew where Abigail's father was; he had been fighting in France but nothing had been heard of him for weeks. The Germans had probably captured him – or he might have been killed.

'At this moment,' Molly said, 'what worries me most is the evacuee boy we're supposed to be getting tonight. I'll probably *hate* him. We don't *need* any more boys in our house. Baby William is enough.'

'I wish we were having one,' Abigail said gloomily. 'But Mum was let off. Because of the trains.' Mrs Murfitt looked after the level-crossing gates at the end of King George Street.

'I'll share him with you,' Molly said generously.

Everything was changing. That afternoon Miss Redway had called the whole school together and told them that 120 evacuees were arriving in the town during the weekend because the Germans were bombing London. They would come on a special train. 'There won't be enough room for them all in the school,' she said. 'So some other places in the town are going to be turned into classrooms for us.'

So, at nine o'clock on Monday, the oldest children were to go to the Methodist Chapel, others to the Salvation Army Hall, and the youngest to the school as usual. Molly and Abigail had held hands under their desks in case they were to be separated. But, no, they were both to go to the Chapel. They didn't mind where they went, as long as they went together.

'Is your dad still doing the same thing?' Abigail asked wistfully, changing the subject.

Molly nodded. 'Yes, driving tanks.'

'Tanks? How many can he drive?'

'Only one at a time,' Molly said and shoved her friend sideways into the dry ditch. 'He could probably drive two at a time if he had to,' she added. She reached for Abigail's hand and pulled her out.

'I wish they'd found him,' Abigail said.

'Who?' Was Abigail talking about her dad?

'The murderer.'

'He'd be hung,' Molly said.

'Good!' Abigail said. But Molly thought that would be something else to shudder about. 'And anyway, you should say *hanged*,' Abigail added.

At Railway Cottage, Abigail's mum was standing by the crossing-gates. Before the War, her dad had opened and closed them when trains came through. Now her mother did it. Sometimes Abigail did it too, but that was illegal. Once she had let Molly do it, and that was even more illegal. Molly was sure the engine driver had glared suspiciously down at her as the train steamed past.

Abigail's mum was talking to old Charlie Leggett. He looked upset and angry. 'Have *you* seen my shovel?' he demanded.

The girls shook their heads. Molly could see there were tears in Charlie's eyes.

'Someone's taken my old shovel,' he said. 'That's been took from my front garden where I left it!' Then he turned and limped away towards his house.

'Come round later?' Molly suggested.

'Yes, I will! I want to see your new boy!' Abigail shouted as she went in with her mum. 'Unless there's an air-raid.'

A few minutes later, Molly approached her home, with its notice outside. *Ely Guesthouse ~ High Class Bed and Breakfast*. It always irritated Molly when she saw it. She liked the 'High Class' part but Ely was twelve miles away and it was inaccurate to call it that. Before the War, lots of people used to visit Great Deeping. Very rich people stayed at the Crown, and fairly rich people stayed at Molly's mum's guesthouse. Those who had hardly any money at all stayed in some caravans in Bunty Fen.

They came for the fishing. The Great Ouse was famous for it. Molly and Abigail called it the Big Mud. But, secretly, Molly liked the big brown river that pushed its way across the flat countryside.

There were still a few occasional visitors, with their fishing-rods and umbrellas and small collapsible chairs. Old men mostly, too old to be called up for the War. They always seemed sad, as if they were remembering the last one.

'Did you come home along Murdered Man Path?'

Molly's mum asked. Molly knew she was being teased, but she corrected her mother anyway. 'It's Dead Man's Way,' she said sternly.

'And is the dead man still there?' Mum asked innocently.

Molly was outraged. 'Of course not! Everyone knows he's in one of the cells at the police station. Lying on a table.'

'Is he really?' her mum said. 'But guess what! We have a proper paying guest coming to stay tomorrow – for a whole month at least.'

This was good news. Molly and her little brother might get some new clothes, and there would be better food for a while. The more ration books there were, the better everyone ate.

'But the evacuee – when is *he* arriving?' Molly said, pulling a long face.

Her mum bent down, took her by the shoulders and looked her in the eyes. 'It'll be all right,' she said. 'We'll manage.'

'I *know*,' Molly wailed. 'But I like it just the way it is. If we can't have Dad here, why do we want some big bossy boy from Bethnal Green?'

'He might be a big handsome heavyweight from Hackney,' Mum said. 'Or a sturdy stalwart from Stepney.'

Friday 20th September ~ afternoon

The boy sighed as he stared out of the carriage window at the massive vertical columns, the glass roof, and the diagonal shafts of weak sunlight.

Liverpool Street Station.

Crowds of children in their school clothes. And grown-ups, looking worried. Mothers mostly, and a few men in uniform. Some railway porters, schoolteachers with lists. Children with gas-masks in awkward boxes. Small cheap suitcases made of cardboard, coloured brown to look like leather.

Faces, faces, faces. Everywhere faces. The children mostly smiling and cheerful. A big adventure – going for a long holiday in the country, riding on a train for the first time. But not the younger ones – they looked worried, scared, holding tight onto older brothers and sisters.

Some of them had been evacuated before, a year ago in 1939. But there had been no bombing after all. So, after a week or two, most of them came back to London. But this time the Germans meant business. The bombers came every night, and the bombing went on for hours.

In Adam's suitcase, there was a brand-new sketchbook together with some pencils. There were three spare pencils tucked down his leg, inside his sock.

No-one had come to see Adam off. His mother worked in the War Department. It was not an especially important job, she said, but she couldn't take time off. His father was in the Fire Service and had hardly been seen since the Blitz had started. In just a few weeks he had become an exhausted and haggard stranger. Gran had come with Adam to the station, but she refused to come onto the platform. She'd had enough station goodbyes in the first War, she said, and she couldn't face any more. So she'd hugged him, and checked that he had everything he needed, in the street outside.

Adam watched his fellow passengers. His classmates, mostly. And a teacher or two. One or two mothers with small babies. Their holiday gaiety vanished almost as soon as the train pulled away from the platform. Waving stopped, windows were shut, faces changed shape.

Homesickness overcame many of them. Smaller children in tears. Miss Waite hurrying along the corridor, checking. Millie Wilson complaining that she had some grit in her eye.

The train stopped at Bethnal Green station and another crowd of children clambered on board, with name-labels and gas-masks and suitcases. They too were smiling and cheerful, as if going on holiday. But when the train left the station, the tears started again.

The same thing happened at Hackney Downs. But when they reached Clapton there had been an air-raid warning and the waiting children had been hurried away to the nearest shelters. The train didn't wait for the raid to be over; it left without them, snaking its way northwards towards Tottenham Hale, full of children, away from the bombing.

Adam peered upwards. Seven planes climbing steeply. High, and too far away for him to identify. His friends saw him watching. They crowded at the window and crouched low on the floor so that they could peer high up. But the planes flew out of sight.

They passed through small villages and towns. At every station the place-names had been removed to confuse the Germans if they invaded.

Out in the country, there was a plane that had crashed in some swampy ground close to the railway track. Messerschmitt 109, with a small swastika on its tail. Part of the fuselage was visible, crumpled and hurt; the rest was buried in the mud. There was a small crowd of onlookers, and a stretcher was being carried across the field from a van in the road. From further along the train, some children could be heard cheering.

Much later, a small city in the country with a big cathedral and a wide river. The first cohort of children climbed down onto the platform. Teachers shouting, giving orders. Local people waiting to welcome them. The others watched with interest as the train pulled away and left them there.

It stopped at another station. More children got out to be left with strangers.

Later, it stopped again for no apparent reason. An enormous flat field with no hedges to define it. And a solitary man leaning on a hoe, watching them. Parallel rows of green things, converging into the distance. Everything in sight was horizontal, except the man with the hoe – and some distant telegraph poles. The man's shadow was long in the evening sun.

Adam opened his suitcase and took out his sketchbook and a pencil. He drew six rectangular frames, freehand. The other children in the compartment watched. They were used to this.

In the first frame, Adam drew a straight line from one side to the other. He nudged the pencil so tinily that they could hardly see – and yet, like magic, the line was transformed into a flat horizon with a minute distant stump of a church tower, and some trees, and a few rooftops.

In the top righthand corner of the sky Adam put six black dots; in the opposite corner was another dot. In the next frame he repeated the horizon, but this time it was lower. The dots were bigger, and had become tiny flat specks, tilted slightly, in formation. In the third frame there was no horizon at all, and the six dots had become six German Stuka dive-bombers, heading straight for the watcher. The other, single, dot was bigger too and was heading straight for the bombers.

'Spitfire,' whispered Nobby Clark.

'No,' Dottie Grayson said. 'Hurricane.' The others murmured their agreement. A solitary Hurricane on patrol.

What was going to happen?

The fourth frame zoomed in on the Hurricane and one of the Stukas – there, before their very eyes. You could *see* their speed. A line of bullets went from the Hurricane direct to its target. At the edge of the frame, the wing-tip of one of the other German planes could just be seen. In the fifth frame, the Stuka streamed down through the sky towards the empty horizon, smoke pouring from it. The sixth picture was at ground level, and showed the dive-bomber crashed vertically into a swamp, with the rear of its fuselage and its tail section protruding from the mud.

The onlookers sighed with appreciation.

Adam hesitated, thought for a moment, and then drew in – high in the righthand corner of the empty sky – a tiny figure parachuting down. There should have been another, but with a brief hardening of the heart Adam left him in the doomed plane.

With a jerk, the train began to move. Adam wrote his initials, small in the bottom corner of the last frame. His teacher had told him he must always do that. He carefully tore the page from his sketchbook. It was passed round for inspection.

The train came to the outskirts of a small town. As it slowed, it passed over a level-crossing. A small crowd of village children stood there, watching the train. One of them, a girl, was clinging dreamily to the crossing-gate, waiting to swing back on it when the train had passed. Then, almost immediately, it stopped at a small country station, with its signs painted black but the letters beneath still legible.

Great Deeping.

'I'm getting out here.'

'You can't! We're not allowed.'

'This ain't the place our lot's supposed to be going to, Swalesey.'

'There'll be a bloomin' great fuss if you do!'

Adam said nothing. He closed the fasteners of his suitcase, adjusted his gas-mask, and opened the carriage window. The door swung open, and as he jumped down he called behind him, 'Dottie! You can keep the picture if you want!'

They were used to that too. Adam Swales always gave his pictures away.

The train steamed north towards Downham Market and King's Lynn. On the quiet country platform there were more than a hundred children. Below, in the station yard, were a bus and two tractors with trailers attached. The bus was quickly full and the first of the trailers was filling up.

Adam joined the crowd. As he shuffled forward with the rest, he looked up into the darkening sky. Bigger than any sky he'd ever seen. With six – no, seven – rooks winging their leisurely way towards the churchyard. In formation. And a solitary approaching plane.

Adam recognised it from pictures. A B24 Liberator, a brand-new non-combat plane with US markings. Fresh from take-off, rising steadily, and heading west. With an unhurried and heavy dignity it was leaving the war-zone of Europe and flying to safety. Where to? he wondered. New York? Washington? Chicago?

A strange arrival, Adam thought.

Carted around on a trailer in an unknown town, stopping at houses as darkness fell. At each house, one of the children was dropped off. Sometimes two together if they were brothers or sisters. A woman from the Women's Voluntary Service was with them, young, efficient, cheerful. At each door, there were explanations and instructions.

It was almost dark when, finally, it was Adam's turn but he could see that the house was bigger than most of the others. There was a notice outside: *Ely Guesthouse*.

A woman on the doorstep, and two girls standing shyly with her. Adam guessed they were about his age. Behind them, a long dark passage, and a light in the depths of the house. Like living in a cave.

'Well, Mrs Barnes, we have one for you. He says his name is Adam Swales. He's not on my list for some reason. There's been some kind of muddle. But it won't make any difference to you, will it? One boy is just like any other boy. We were expecting more, to be honest. But they haven't all come.'

Mrs Barnes took a few steps into the street and took

Adam's case while he jumped to the ground. Then she shook his hand and said she hoped he would be happy with them.

Who *are* these people? Adam thought.

'There's one important rule, Mrs Barnes. Please make sure that Adam writes to his family tomorrow – to let them know where he is staying and that he is all right.'

The door was shut behind him and Adam found himself being led along a passage in almost total blackness. There were unevennesses in the floor which his feet didn't know about. He sensed that they passed a couple of large empty rooms, one on each side.

One of the girls was chattering. 'I'm Abigail. I don't live here. Molly lives here. I live at the crossing-house by the railway. I saw you lot come in.'

Someone's hand guided him from behind, round a corner and into a large kitchen. He had never seen a room like this. Low ceiling, huge stove, cupboards and shelves on every wall. Cluttered but spacious. How strange it all was. These people were cave-dwellers. He had come to live among aliens.

But the table was familiar. A big steel air-raid shelter, with metal grilles fixed on all four sides. They had one at home. They hadn't been given an Anderson shelter because their backyard wasn't big enough to put it in. Instead, his father had installed the table-shelter with some of his workmates. You could unhook the grilles so that there was space for your legs when you sat at the table. 'It won't stand a direct hit, but it will protect from falling masonry,' his dad had said. 'We'll be like animals in a cage.'

'Girls, show Adam where his room is. When you come down, Adam, there will be something for you to eat.'

He worked out the two girls. The quiet one lived here but it was Abigail, her friend, who did most of the talking. She was excited and happy, explaining where the big breakfast room was, and the bathroom and the lavatory, and which parts of the house were set aside for paying guests. Molly, the other one, was watchful.

Alone in his room, he put out the light, pulled back the curtain and opened the window. Below him was the street. Not a light to be seen – total blackout. He was used to that; it was like that back home. But the darkness there was busy, full of noise and people and vehicles. Here the street was empty and silent. The sky, too, was peaceful and still.

Adam sighed. He closed the window and began the journey back down to the kitchen. He took with him his sketchbook and a pencil. I need a map for this house, he thought.

A plate piled high awaited him. 'We had ours earlier,' Mrs Barnes said. 'I kept this warm for you.' Meat and Yorkshire pudding, with peas, sprouts, mashed potatoes and gravy. There was a slight dryness all over where it had been kept hot in the oven, but under that it was delicious.

The girls sat at the table opposite him, with scissors and paste.

'What are you doing?' Apart from a few thankyous, this was the first time he had spoken.

'Molly's sorting out her Rupert stories,' Abigail said. 'I'm helping.'

There was a big pile of pages torn from past copies of the *Daily Express* and Molly was cutting out the Rupert Bear stories, arranging them for glueing in a scrapbook.

'I'm saving them for my baby brother,' Molly said. 'For when he's older.'

Adam found himself looking directly into her eyes. 'I used to read them,' he said. 'There used to be two pictures every day, not just one.'

'There's only one now – because of the War,' Molly said quietly.

Adam opened his sketchbook and drew a frame. Abigail watched, wide-eyed and puzzled. In Adam's mind Rupert Bear was standing with a bren gun, under a night sky and taking aim at a passing Messerschmitt.

One of the Rupert episodes was missing. The girls couldn't find number 32. Adam joined in the search. There were old copies of the *Daily Express* all over the table, in disorderly piles on chairs, and on the floor.

But number 32 was nowhere to be found and Molly, in spite of not wanting to seem babyish, had tears in her eyes. Abigail, knowing her friend, explained her to

Adam. 'If one bit is missing, it spoils the whole story,' she said. 'It's like jigsaw puzzles.'

Adam took up his pencil. 'What happens in the missing bit?' he asked Molly.

Molly found numbers 31 and 33 and studied them. 'Well, not much,' she admitted. 'In 31 Rupert is walking up a hill, searching for his friend Algy Pug. In 33, he's found him and they are talking.'

Adam studied the two episodes. 'Can you write out the missing bit?'

'I can make it up,' Molly said. But she asked Abigail to write it because she could do writing which was neat and really small. Adam showed her where to write it in his sketchbook.

Mystified, Molly dictated to Abigail:

Rupert hurries to the top of the hill and sees Algy in the distance. He is overjoyed to see his friend and shouts and waves to him. Algy shouts 'Hurrah! I've seen the Moon Imp!'

Adam drew a small frame beside the words. He took a pencil from his sock, and a penknife from his pocket, and delicately made the point as sharp as a pin. Then he sketched in clear black lines a picture of Rupert Bear, perfect, seen from behind, coming over the brow of a hill, one arm waving and both feet clear of the ground as he ran. The country was wooded and Algy could be seen in the distance at the bottom of the hill, tiny, with his arms in the air. Fat round clouds floated across the sky. Adam finished off by shading in the trees.

He cut the picture and text from his book to match the size of the others. 'It's not the original,' he said. 'But it fits.'

Abigail found ten different ways of saying how wonderful she thought the drawing was. Molly simply said 'Thanks.'

Adam was already beginning his own Rupert Bear story. *Rupert and the Messerschmitts.* A war story, he thought. He stored the idea away in his head for use later.

Adam sat up in bed, listening. The faint wailing of a distant air-raid siren travelled across the Fens. Barely a minute later another siren joined in, loud and much closer. Probably only two streets away.

Nothing was to be seen from the bedroom window. Adam could sense the people – in the town, on distant farms and in scattered cottages. He could *see* them, crouching quietly in the dark and lying still, hoping they would be unnoticed as the enemy flew overhead.

A knock on his door. Molly in pale pink pyjamas. 'Mum says we have to get in the shelter.' She looked sleepy, unhurried.

'Listen!' he said. 'They're Dorniers.'

Molly squinted at him sleepily. 'What?'

The low purposeful roar of the approaching bombers was unutterably sinister.

'They're called flying pencils,' Adam whispered.

'Oh.' Molly left his room and set off towards the stairs. Adam followed. 'Because of their shape.'

In the big kitchen, Molly crawled on all fours into the cave under the shelter-table. Adam followed the soles of her feet. Mrs Barnes had eiderdowns laid out for lying on, and there were rugs and pillows. 'Molly,' she said, 'take Baby William.'

She passed the baby into the shelter and went away. The bombers overhead seemed close enough to slice off rooftops and chimneys as they passed. There was a climax of noise, a prolonged intensive roar.

Molly's mum returned with a tin of biscuits. She passed them to Molly and hurriedly crawled in herself, closing the metal grille behind her.

'Do they come every night?' Adam said into the darkness.

'They did in the summer. We've had a bit of a lull lately – when they turned their attention to London.'

'They sometimes bomb the dummy aerodrome,' Molly said. 'Over near Welney.'

'Dummy aerodrome? What's that?'

'A decoy. A trick to make the Germans bomb that instead of the real airfields. They have planes made of plywood, and everything. I've seen it.'

'Molly, you're not supposed to say that sort of thing. It's top secret and there's a War on. How many times do you have to be told?'

'Adam's not a German spy!' Molly said.

The Dorniers passed westwards and left the night silent again.

'We'll hear them later, on their way back,' Molly said. 'That's when they drop any bombs they've got left.'

Adam thought: I am in a sort of bed, under a sort of table. With a family of complete strangers, in a strange house, in a strange town, in a strange countryside. He thought of home, where the air-raids were noisier, with screaming dive-bombers, falling sticks of bombs, distant thudding explosions, collapsing walls, incendiaries, and fire-engines and ambulances clanging through the streets. Who would be getting the worst of it tonight? Bethnal Green? Hackney? The City?

'We've had a murder,' Molly said. 'Abigail and me are going to solve it. You can help us if you like.'

Adam frowned in the darkness.

What an extraordinary thing to say! Was she being serious?

Saturday 21ˢᵗ September ~ morning

The murder was incomprehensible. An impossible thought. Every night, enemy airmen flew over England intent upon killing thousands of people. Yet this one murder, this single death, stuck in the throat. It was unnatural, unthinkable.

But Molly thought about it all the time.

She was trying to explain this to Abigail on their way home from the shops. Every Saturday morning, they did errands for both their mothers. Molly's mum sometimes needed more shopping because of running a guesthouse, but they shared the work equally. And the wages. A shilling each.

'It's stuck in my mind,' Molly said. 'I can't get rid of it.'

'We need to find out who did it,' Abigail said. 'Then it wouldn't worry you any more.'

Molly shifted the shopping-basket from her left hand to her right. It was heavy and made the inside of her hand sore. It bumped against her leg as she walked.

'Do you think murderers should be hung?' Abigail asked.

Molly corrected her. '*Hanged*,' she said.

'All right! *Hanged*. It was *me* that taught *you* that! But do you?'

'I don't know,' Molly said doubtfully.

'Well, I do! And you should know what you think. It's an important matter.'

'Is it?'

'Well, it's important for the person they're going to hang. Everyone should have an opinion about it.'

'Well, I haven't got one.'

'At Sunday School, Miss Milson says everyone should have opinions.'

Molly was suddenly angry. 'Well, she's wrong! I'm not grown up yet. I don't have to have opinions! It's not my *job* to have opinions.'

'Well, whose is it then?'

'Other people's,' Molly said lamely. 'Judges and policemen and prime ministers. And the king. It's *their* job, it's not mine. I'll get opinions when I'm grown up.'

Molly always got cross when Abigail went on about Sunday School. She went to a different one. It was the only activity where they went to different places. Molly hated the Methodist Sunday School because she didn't go there.

Still, they made friends again quickly. They always did.

'What do you think of your evacuee boy?'

Abigail sounded wistful. Molly considered and said, 'He's OK, I think.' And he *listens*, she added inwardly.

'Did he go in the shelter with you last night?'

Molly nodded.

'What were his pyjamas like?'

Molly looked confused. 'I don't know,' she said helplessly. 'Blue, I think.'

'But were they *clean*?'

'Yes, I think so. How should *I* know?'

'Molly Barnes, you're *useless*! He's good at drawing Rupert Bear. I'll say that for him.' Abigail sounded just like her mother. She didn't know that, but Molly did.

'I told him about the murder,' Molly said. She hesitated and then added: 'I told him he could help us find the person who did it.'

There was just the slightest pause before Abigail asked her why.

'I don't know,' Molly said. 'I just did.'

Molly knew that she had upset Abigail. She also knew that Abigail didn't want another quarrel. So it was up to her to prevent it. 'I'm sorry,' she said. 'I should have asked you first.'

'Oh, well. I daresay we can find a use for him,' Abigail said.

Then Molly knew it was all right. But the fact of the murder was still there. That was not all right. It was in her mind, unshiftable, like a piece of grit in her eye.

There was a man crossing the street towards them. 'Excuse me! I wonder if you could give me some directions.'

The girls stopped and waited.

'I'm looking for the Ely Guesthouse. Could you tell me how to get there?'

Molly and Abigail stood silent, taking him in. He was large, middle-aged, well-dressed and grey-haired, with a friendly face. He was not in uniform.

'Now why,' said the stranger, 'should a perfectly innocent question from a perfectly innocent person cause such consternation?'

'Oh, we're not consternated,' Abigail said. 'It's just a strange coincidence, that's all.'

'What is?'

'Molly lives there. It's her mum who runs the guesthouse.' Abigail was excited. Whenever there was a coincidence, she thought the universe was speaking to her.

'Is that correct?' the man asked Molly.

Molly nodded. She liked his eyes. 'You can come with us if you like,' she said. 'It's only just round the next bend.'

The stranger was relieved. 'I'm very tired,' he admitted. 'It's a long way from the station, and there was no taxi.' Then there was a discussion about how they could help him with his luggage. But, since they had their shopping, there was little they could do.

'I can take your umbrella,' Abigail suggested. 'Then you'll have two hands to carry with.'

Abigail tried swinging the flapping umbrella beside her, as if it were a walking-stick. But it was too long for that, or she was not long enough. She finished up with it over her shoulder, marching like a soldier with a rifle.

Later, they all sat around the big shelter-table in the kitchen. Adam, Molly, Abigail, Mrs Barnes and the new guest. Dinner was fried corned beef, with bubble-and-squeak and fried eggs.

Adam had finished his letter home. It was not really a letter, just a page torn from his sketchbook, with a picture. When he saw Abigail looking at it, he passed it to her, and she shared it with Molly – a cow, a horse, and a pig, all standing on their hind legs, and aiming catapults at a passing German fighter-plane. A cockerel stood on a gatepost waving a Union Jack in its beak. The pilot's head stuck out of the cockpit, with an expression of terror on his face and his hands up in a gesture of surrender. Underneath Adam had written: *Down in the country we are all doing our bit to defeat the invaders.*

Mrs Barnes wondered how his parents would react to such a message. 'They'll know what it means,' Adam said calmly.

The visitor had put them all at their ease. Usually with new ones there was shyness at first. Sometimes it stayed all through their visit. But not with this one. 'My name,' he said, 'is Harold Cuthbertson. But that's a horrible mouthful and ever since I was a boy people have called me Cuffey. I prefer that. So please call me Cuffey.'

Molly's mum was about to say that she thought they had better stick with his proper name. But he was too quick for her. 'On the count of three, all say Cuffey in unison!' Then – before anyone could protest – he said: 'One! Two! *Three!*

Obligingly, everyone muttered 'Cuffey'. Then they all laughed and their embarrassment was done with. Cuffey turned to the big black cat sitting on a spare chair next to him. 'You too,' he said, and Sooty obligingly miaowed.

Everyone laughed. Molly's arm leaned against Abigail's in a companionable sort of way. Under the table, their bare feet were tucked in the pillows used during air-raids.

'Delicious meal,' Cuffey said. 'Such a profusion of eggs!'

'We keep chickens,' Molly said.

'So do we,' Abigail said. Molly knew Abigail was hoping for a second dinner when she got home. She thought she might go and help her to eat it. It was convenient that the two mums did their Saturday dinners at different times.

'Are you here on holiday?' Molly's mum asked him.

'No, I'm doing some surveying work for the War Department. On level crossings and bridges. Just started, actually. I'm new at it.'

'Places to blow up if the Germans invade?' Abigail

asked. She felt she had a right to know because she lived beside one.

'I hope it won't come to that,' Cuffey said.

There was a short silence, full of thoughts of an enemy invasion.

'I am one of many men at an awkward age,' Cuffey said. 'I was called up for the last War but I am too old for this one.'

'Do you feel left out?' Molly asked him.

She could feel Abigail's shocked disapproval. *You shouldn't ask personal questions!*

But Cuffey took the question seriously. 'Well, yes, sometimes I do. But, there are some advantages. Surveying bridges is not as frightening as being in the front line.'

A man admitting he had been frightened! Another surprise for Abigail.

After dinner, when they were all sitting around the big table in a chatty sort of way with cups of tea, they received two visitors – two policemen, one in plain clothes and the other a sergeant in uniform.

'I am Detective Chief Superintendent Munnings, ma'am. You should call me *Mister* Munnings. And this is Sergeant . . . '

'Sergeant Bly, ma'am,' said the man in uniform. He and Molly's mum used to sit next to each other in primary school.

'You've come about the murder,' Mrs Barnes said.

Molly and Abigail sat up straight in their seats. Being visited by a Detective Chief Superintendent gave them an important feeling. Adam just stared: so there really *had* been a murder.

'You, sir,' the policeman said. 'Do you mind telling me who you are and why you're here?'

The new visitor told them his name, showed his identity card, and explained why he was in Great Deeping. 'I am also checking the local footpaths,' he added.

'Footpaths,' said Mr Munnings thoughtfully. 'Not a very vital activity in Wartime, is it?'

'The first thing that an airman will look for,' Cuffey said, 'if he is unlucky enough to have to bail out of his plane, is a footpath that will take him somewhere. Whether he is British or German.'

Detective Chief Superintendent Munnings looked skeptical.

'Footpaths hold this country together,' Cuffey added. 'Like tiny veins in the human body.' But Mr Munnings glanced across to his sergeant and ever so slightly raised his eyebrows.

Molly and Abigail both saw this. They communicated indignation to each other.

'And you, young man. I suppose you're an evacuee?'

Adam nodded. Yes, he was, and yes, his home was in the East End of London.

'Mrs Barnes,' the Chief Superintendent said, 'I know

you've already been questioned about guests who stayed here in the days before the murder. I have been put in charge now, and I'd like you to try to recall any enquiries you might have had, by post or by telephone, in the days *before* the crime. Can you remember any?'

'I don't get many enquiries now,' Molly's mum said. 'So it's not difficult to remember them. No, apart from Mr Cuthbertson here, I've had no enquiries from people I didn't know already – previous visitors. Mostly they were ringing up to say they wouldn't be coming this year.'

'Pity,' said the Chief Superintendent. 'I was hoping there might be a lead there. I'm afraid we don't yet know anything about the killer.'

'*We* do!' Abigail said.

Mr Munnings looked at Abigail in amusement.

'*You* do?'

'It's not a *he*. It's a one-legged French woman,' Abigail announced.

'That would be rather unusual,' Mr Munnings said cautiously.

Now everyone was looking at Abigail. Abigail had not got Molly's approval about this. She glanced at her and Molly nodded.

'We've been looking for clues,' Abigail said. 'To help you.'

The detective stared. 'Molly,' he said to Abigail, 'children should never – I repeat, *never* – interfere with the scene of a crime.'

There was no response. 'And I hope you, Abigail,' he said to Molly, 'appreciate that too. Police work must be left to policemen.'

Abigail ignored this. She always ignored lectures. 'There were little holes in the mud on the footpath,' she said. 'As if they were made by a high-heeled shoe. But they were too far apart to be footprints – unless she was hopping on one leg. Which we think is impossible.'

'Well observed! We saw those too,' The Chief Superintendent said.

Everyone laughed. No-one was taking the one-legged killer seriously.

'But why did you say she was French?' the Sergeant asked.

Then – from the top shelf of the dresser – Molly produced a flat tin biscuit-box, with a label stuck on the lid, on which was written CLUES. From it she took a small piece of paper, dirty and creased, and handed it to the Superintendent.

'It's a bill from a café in Paris,' Molly said. 'And it's dated 3rd February this year.'

'Where did you find this?' The atmosphere in the room had changed.

The Chief Superintendent passed the scrap of paper to Sergeant Bly, who read it aloud: *Café Renoir, Rue Lepic, Paris.*

'We found it on the footpath, not far from where the body was found,' Abigail said. 'Your men missed it.'

'So they did,' said the detective thoughtfully. 'What else have you got in that tin?'

Molly showed him. It was empty.

'I'll have to ask you to let me keep this bill,' the Superintendent said. 'You've done very well, I must say.' He looked hard at Molly and Abigail.

Mrs Barnes then voiced the question that was in everyone's mind. 'But how could anyone who was in Paris in February get to England when there's a War on?'

'Precisely, ma'am!' said Abigail in a deep voice. She was being Sherlock Holmes.

When the policemen had left, Cuffey asked if there was a cinema in Great Deeping, and what was showing there.

'*Rebecca*, with Laurence Olivier and Joan Fontaine,' Abigail said at once.

'Well, why don't we all go tonight?' Cuffey said. 'I would like to make it my treat.'

'Me too?' Abigail asked.

'Yes, of course, if your mother says it's all right.'

The girls cheered. But Mrs Barnes had already seen the film; she went out with her friends every Thursday. And Adam didn't think it was his kind of film.

'Come with us,' Molly said quietly. 'And we'll come with you to see the *Charlie Chan* film next week.'

'*Charlie Chan in Panama*,' Abigail said.

'Do you go to the pictures a lot?' Adam said.

'We go to everything,' Abigail said happily. 'Whether we think we'll like it or not.'

'I'll come,' Adam said, cheering a little. 'Will you show me the place where the murder happened?'

'Yes! Let's go now! Come on!'

'There!' Abigail said triumphantly, pointing at a dry ditch.

Adam looked. Long grass and other growing things. Nothing else.

They showed him the holes in the footpath. 'It had rained that day,' Abigail explained.

The holes had set in the dried mud. Too far apart for an ordinary walker. 'She could have been running and lost one of her shoes,' he suggested.

They hadn't thought of that. So they searched for a missing shoe. Unsuccessfully.

'It's no good,' Abigail moaned.

'We're at a disadvantage,' Adam said. 'You can bet your last sixpence the police won't tell us about *their* clues. But they expect *us* to tell them about *ours*.'

Molly glanced at him. He knew it was because he had said *we* and *us* and *ours*. Was she pleased?

But they did find something. At the end of the footpath, where it turned into Pond Lane, there was a stile. In the tangle of brambles to one side of it was the next clue.

Perhaps.

A thin grubby strip of black elastic, about three inches long, with a small metal ring at one end. The other end had been torn from something.

'What use is a clue if you don't know what it is?' Abigail said.

They joked about knicker-elastic, but they knew it had nothing to do with knickers. Are we playing a game? Adam wondered. Or is this real?

'It's not long enough to strangle anybody with,' Abigail said.

'He wasn't strangled. He was shot.'

'It's a long way from the where the body was,' Molly said doubtfully. 'Perhaps it doesn't count as a clue.'

'Into the CLUES box it goes!' Abigail said firmly. 'What do you think, Adam?'

Adam agreed. He was game for anything.

'What's happening over there?' Adam was pointing at some farm buildings about a mile away across the fields. He thought he could see a soldier with a machine-gun.

'That's our prisoner-of-war camp,' Abigail said.

Adam stared with interest.

'They're living in some old chicken-sheds belonging to Mr Morton,' Abigail said. 'It was Mr Morton's aunt who found the corpse – old Miss Morton.'

'Chicken-sheds?'

'Well, they're building some Nissen huts for them,' Molly explained. 'But for the time being . . . '

'Actually,' Abigail said, 'it's the prisoners who are doing the building.'

'They don't look very well-guarded,' Adam said thoughtfully. 'How many are there?'

Abigail didn't know. About thirty, she guessed. 'Some of them do jobs in the town.'

Adam was amazed.

'One of them was a blacksmith in Germany. He goes every day to help old Joe Proudfoot in his forge.'

'I hope they finish building their huts before the cold weather starts,' Molly said.

'They *deserve* to be cold!' Abigail said.

'What's *that* place?' Adam asked.

'That's Paradise Barn,' Molly said.

'Our barn,' Abigail added.

'*Your* barn?'

'Well, we go there. We'll show you some time.'

Abigail was enthusiastic. Molly wasn't so sure. She thought they should keep their barn for themselves.

There were small groups of evacuee children in the streets of the town. Those who had been allowed out had gone in search of their friends. They stood on street corners, studied shop-windows, told each other about the families they were staying with. They were restless – excited and bored at the same time. Someone arrived with a tennis ball and a kick-about got going in the Main Street.

'Are they from your school?' Abigail asked. Adam shook his head. He didn't know any of them. His schoolmates were wandering the streets of King's Lynn.

Adam said he would like to see the blacksmith's forge.

'What for?' demanded Abigail.

'I'd like to see a German prisoner.'

So the girl's took him to the forge. There was often a group of schoolchildren at the door, peering in, watching the fiery work of Joe Proudfoot. Today, though, the German stood there in his drab prisoner's uniform, leaning against the door-frame, gloomily watching the passers-by.

Adam was amazed that he was allowed to move about freely. He was supposed to be a prisoner. 'He could just walk away,' he said in disbelief.

'He couldn't walk home to Germany,' Abigail said. 'We're an island.'

They had stopped on the other side of the street. 'I bet he's capable of murder,' Abigail said quietly.

'Why?'

'Well, look at his face!'

'He's just unhappy,' Molly said.

As they stared, the German winked at them – slowly, the rest of his face remaining expressionless and unchanging.

They felt embarrassed and awkward, standing there and staring. So they raced off, glad to leave the German prisoner to his own devices.

A huge noise approached, like nothing Adam had ever heard. A steam-roller, he thought for a moment.

He had seen nothing like it. Massive iron wheels were grinding into the surface of the road, pistons pushed and yielded, steam hissed and spat, fly-wheels spun in the sunlight. There was a powerful smell of coal, smoke and hot metal. It was a traction engine, with all the powerful strength of a steam locomotive but none of its promise of speed. It was towing an enormous contraption – an ancient wooden dinosaur-object on metal wheels, painted salmon pink and as long as a bus.

'That's Farmer Summerley's traction engine,' Abigail said.

'And that's his threshing machine,' Molly explained.

A young man stood high on the platform driving the traction engine, and a little girl of about seven stood with him. She flicked back her plaits loftily and looked proudly around her as she wiped grease from her arms with a rag.

A small house stood back from the road, with a tiny front garden. The driver drew the engine close to the garden wall. With a sigh and a hiss of steam, the great engine came to a clumsy standstill and stood there boiling and hissing softly.

'That's Mrs Weathergreen's house,' Molly said.

A neat old lady stood in the garden. She was looking

up and talking to the young man high above her in the cab of the traction engine.

Out came Adam's sketch-pad and pencil. He worked with quick movements, looking sharply up at the engine and sharply down again at the paper.

Abigail nudged Molly. Molly said, 'Can we see?'

'Later,' Adam said. It was hardly more than a grunt.

Mrs Weathergreen's conversation with the young man did not last long. She went indoors, the traction engine and the threshing machine moved away down the street, and suddenly everywhere was quiet.

Adam sighed and put away his drawing things.

'Have you heard about Mrs Weathergreen's flower-press?' Abigail asked Molly.

'Everybody's heard about that!' Molly said.

'I haven't,' Adam said.

'She collects wild flowers,' Molly said. 'She's famous. She's written a book about it – and she had an amazing flower-press, as big as a suitcase, made of mahogany and with brass fittings.'

'Someone stole it,' Abigail added.

'It's a shame!' Molly liked Mrs Weathergreen.

'Her husband used to be the vicar.'

'Why isn't he now?'

Abigail looked shocked. 'Because he's dead!'

'Why would anyone want to steal a flower-press?' Adam said.

'There's been a lot of stealing,' Molly explained. 'Someone took poor old Charlie Leggett's shovel too.'

'He makes such a *fuss*,' Abigail grumbled. 'It's only an old shovel with a broken handle. I know! I've seen it.'

Why would anyone want a shovel with a broken handle? Adam wondered. And where did Charlie Leggett belong in this complicated life he'd walked into?

'He can't help it,' Molly said. Then she added: 'His granddad told him it once belonged to Alfred the Great.'
Abigail stopped and stared.

'It's true! He did! He said it got broken when the Vikings brought their boats up the river. Alfred whacked one of them on the head with it.'

'And he *believes* that?'

They heard – faintly from across the flat fields – Littleport's air-raid siren. They stopped and paid attention, knowing what was coming. Only a few seconds later, their own siren started up. And then came the one in Downham Market, wailing from five miles away.

'More Vikings,' Abigail whispered. The two girls held hands and raced for home. Adam ran with them, gazing skywards longingly. Then he tripped over an iron shoe-scraper and Abigail grabbed his hand too. 'To prevent any more accidents,' she said to Molly.

She sounds exactly like her mum, Molly thought.

The air-raid was a false alarm and the all-clear sounded almost immediately. Afterwards, Adam went to his room and stayed there for about an hour. When he came down to the kitchen, with his sketch-book, he found the girls chatting contentedly about films.

Molly had expected a hard black drawing of a traction engine. The engine was there sure enough, lightly sketched and accurate as far she could tell. But it was a background only. The drawing was interested in the three faces: the beautiful girl with dark eyes and long plaits; the young man, broad-chested and dark, smiling brightly down; and the old lady, looking eagerly up at him, serious and tender. Like three people in an old story, Molly thought.

This was no Rupert Bear drawing, or cartoon of farmyard animals aiming at enemy planes. This was different.

Abigail looked at Molly with her eyes wide with surprise. Molly looked at Adam. Adam was already thinking about something else.

'Is Abigail coming round tonight?' Mum asked.

'No,' Molly said. 'She's been sent to bed early with no supper.'

'What's she done this time?'

'She sang a song while she was sitting on the lav.'

Molly was kneeling on the floor, changing Baby William's nappy. She didn't mind doing this if it wasn't too disgusting. This one was just wet and she dumped it in a bucket. Adam was playing football somewhere with some children he had got to know.

'That seems a bit severe, even for Abigail's mum. What was the song?'

Molly sat back on her heels and began to sing. 'Hitler has only *got one ball* . . . ' she sang happily.

'*Molly!*' her Mum said sharply.

'What?'

'That's very rude.'

Molly knelt back and sighed. '*Why*?' she wailed in despair. 'It doesn't seem rude to me.'

Mum came over and knelt down beside her. 'Because we don't talk about that sort of thing. Let alone sing songs about it.'

'*What* sort of thing?' Molly felt exasperated.

'Men's –'

Molly saw that her Mum couldn't even say it. 'What's wrong with talking about balls?' she said.

'They're not footballs, or tennis balls,' Mum said.

'What are they then?'

Using Baby William to demonstrate with, Mum explained what balls were. She tried to explain why they mattered but she got muddled. Molly noticed that her Mum's face and neck were bright red. Then she began to feel that she was blushing too, and she felt hot. This is a *hot-making* subject, she thought with interest.

'All right,' Molly said. 'But why has Hitler only got one?'

'I'm sure he has two, just like other men,' her mum said.

This really confused Molly. 'Then why does the song say he's only got one?' she demanded angrily.

'I think it's a way of saying that he isn't a proper man – and he has to start wars and kill people to make up for it. It's a way of making him seem ridiculous – and Himmler and Goebbels as well,' she added.

So Mum knows the rest of the song too, Molly thought. She sighed but said no more. Mum knew the song, Molly and Abigail knew the song, Abigail's mum must know about the song, and they all knew about men's balls (except for Baby William, who didn't yet know that he had any).

But, for some reason, it was rude to talk about it.

Molly finished cleaning little William and fetched Mum's shopping basket. In it she put a length of string, a generous slice of home-made pork pie, an apple and a small bottle of Mum's ginger beer. These she took to Abigail's house. While the 6.50 from Liverpool Street was due to come through, she called up to her friend's bedroom. Abigail pushed up the window and leaned out. There were always garden tools lying around Abigail's mum's garden, and Molly tied one end of the string to a rake and reached it up to Abigail, who untied it and pulled up the basket.

'Thanks,' she whispered. She seemed quite cheerful, Molly thought. She knew that Abigail had a supply of comics hidden under her mattress ready for such occasions.

Molly walked slowly home in the twilight, thinking about Baby William's balls. Then she heard the air-raid warnings wailing across the flat fields – and she raced for home.

But the air-raid warning was another false alarm and the all-clear sounded almost before Molly had joined Adam under the shelter. So the shelter became a kitchen table again and she settled down there to read her latest *Biggles* book. Adam began folding old copies of the *Daily Express* and putting them aside for fire-lighting. He occasionally stopped to read a news item. Some pages had a square hole cut out of them.

Molly felt his sudden excitement as if she had been struck.

What?

He was poring over a small feature on the back of the *Rupert Bear* page. He slid the paper across to her and pointed. Molly read the small cramped print.

ART THEFT Two valuable paintings were stolen from the Louvre Museum in Paris on 14th June, the day that German troops entered the city. It is believed that the thieves deliberately took advantage of the confusion caused by the Nazis' arrival. The best-known is a painting by Camille Pissarro, exhibited first in 1882 and entitled Vue de Pontoise. The other

There the item came to an end because *Rupert Bear* had been cut out and was now pasted into Molly's scrapbook. But there was a picture of the missing painting by Pissarro, fuzzy and grey.

'I've got a copy of that in my art book,' Adam whispered.

Molly was confused. 'What art book?'

'Back home,' Adam said.

The paper was dated 18th June. Adam continued to gaze at it, transfixed, and Molly studied him, puzzled.

Sergeant Bly came to visit that evening. The Chief Superintendent was not with him, and so he and Mrs

Barnes called each other Michael and Mary.

'You've come about the murder?'

'No,' said Michael Bly. 'I've come about that young man over there.' He was looking severely at Adam.

'Adam? Why? What's he done?'

'He shouldn't be here at all, Mary, that's what. He got off at the wrong station and mixed in with our lot of evacuees. He *should*'ve gone on to King's Lynn.'

'Is this true, Adam?'

Adam nodded.

'But why?' Molly's mum asked. 'Did you make a mistake?'

'No,' Adam said. 'I liked the look of Great Deeping. So I got off the train.'

Molly was wide-eyed. When she was in trouble, she did one of two things. Sometimes she lied, if she thought she could get away with it. Sometimes – in an outburst of remorse and self-reproach – she poured out the truth in a rush, longing for forgiveness. Abigail did neither of these things; she just stared, saying nothing, and waiting for the storm to blow over. But Adam! He coolly admitted what he'd done – without shame, without lying, without rudeness, without any distress at all.

Molly didn't know it could be done like that.

'You shouldn't have done that, Adam,' Mrs Barnes said. 'That sort of thing causes a lot of trouble.' Then, to the sergeant, 'What happens now, Michael? I hope you're not going to take him away.'

'Well, by rights, he ought to be sent to King's Lynn.'

'But it's such a waste. I have plenty of room here for at least one evacuee.'

'Oh, you'd have one all right, Mary. They're still coming out of London in their hundreds. We could find you a different one.'

Molly's mum was moving across the kitchen with a tea-pot in one hand. She stopped behind Adam's chair and briefly rested her other hand on his head. 'But we don't want a different one. We like *this* one.'

Adam was pleased. Molly was not certain how she knew this, but she was sure. It's going to be all right, she thought.

'Well, we'll leave it like that then, Mary. I can't just put him on the train to Lynn because he might decide to go somewhere different. And I can't spare the time to take him there myself. But you, young man! No more tricks of that sort, understand?'

Adam nodded and the sergeant got up to go. 'By the way,' he said, 'we've had a bit of a lead on the murder.'

They were all ears.

'I don't suppose I ought to tell you really,' the sergeant said. 'It's just that we now know who the victim was. His name was Dufour. He was a French art-dealer.'

Molly thought she might ask Cuffey about balls. She trusted him not to confuse her. However, whenever there was an opportunity, she was too shy and the question never got asked.

But she did tell Abigail about it, and Abigail claimed to have known all along.

'You didn't!' Molly said. 'You said the same thing when we were six and I told you Father Christmas wasn't real.'

Abigail stared. Then she said, 'I wonder if Father Christmas has got balls.'

Softly they began to sing in unison. 'Santa has only *got one ball . . .* '

When she got home, Adam had gone out. He and a couple of Great Deeping boys planned to make a book called *How to Spot Enemy Aircraft.* The two Great Deeping boys had the technical know-how, and Adam would do the illustrations.

Molly felt at a loose end. So, when Cuffey asked her if she would like to go to the pictures with him again, she jumped at the chance and said yes – if Abigail could come too, and as long as Mum didn't mind. Mum didn't.

Abigail's mum said she would be pleased to see the back of Abigail. So they went.

Afterwards, they came out of the cinema into the dark street and set off for home. Molly and Abigail walked one on each side of Cuffey.

'Well, what did you think of the film?' he asked them. 'We have to discuss it. It's the law.'

'It was OK,' Abigail said cautiously.

'But . . . ?' Cuffey said.

Molly voiced their misgivings about it. 'It was *him*, Buster, the hero.'

'What was wrong with him?'

'He fell in love with every pretty girl he met!' Molly said.

'He did, that's true,' said Cuffey.

'He fell in love with eight different girls,' Molly went on. 'And they fell in love with him because he was good at tap-dancing!'

'And then he went back to the first one and fell in love with her all over again!' Abigail added.

'Do men really do that?' Molly asked.

'I'll tell you something,' Cuffey said.

They paid attention. 'We all – men and women – have enough love in us to fall in love three times in our lives. Just three.'

'But . . .'

'After that, it's just pretence.'

'But you're supposed to fall in love only once,' Molly said.

'For some people, that's true. But never more than three times.'

'But the man in the film . . . ?'

'That wasn't love. Not a full-blown passion.' The girls silently transmitted to each other in the darkness – interest, amusement, disbelief. Nobody ever talked to them about passion.

'Passion?' Abigail said. 'What's passion?' Mischief was sparking around her like electricity.

Cuffey said nothing for a few moments. 'I can't explain it to you,' he said eventually. 'Passion marches to a grown-up drum – and your stride isn't yet big enough.'

Abigail lengthened her stride and stepped out. Molly just felt gloomy.

Cuffey would say no more, and soon they arrived at the level-crossing, where Abigail's mum was opening the gates for the 9.45 train to Liverpool Street.

Alone with Cuffey, Molly said, 'Cuffey?'

He looked down at her.

'Have *you* been in love three times?' she said.

'Four,' Cuffey said.

'But *you* said – '

'I know. But the first time didn't count. I was only an apprentice lover.'

'How old were you?'

'Ten. But the other three times were real. So, alas, no

more loving for me. It's all used up!' He put his hand on the top of her head as if to steer her through the darkness, towards home.

'What was her name?'

'Which one?'

'The first one – when you were only ten.'

'Hélène.'

'Helen?'

'No – *Hélène*.'

'Was she French, then?'

'She still is.'

Molly wanted to ask him more, but she wasn't exactly sure what she wanted to find out, so she said nothing at all. But when they reached home, she hugged her mother hard, thinking all the time, '*You've* only been in love *once*. I *know*!'

When the hugging was finished, Mrs Barnes had some news. 'We're having another guest,' she said. 'A young woman. Someone phoned from the Air Ministry.'

'Oh, *no*!'

'Oh, *yes*. Apparently this person will be coming and going unexpectedly. But they're going to pay me to keep her room permanently available for her.'

'But I don't want anyone else here,' Molly said. Her bottom lip stuck out like a scoop.

'Molly, you never do!'

'I know. I like it the way it is.' Then she added: 'Except for Dad not being here.'

'Molly, this is a guesthouse. It's my *job* to have visitors here!'

'I don't like it when things keep changing.'

There was a photo of her father on the shelf over the fireplace. She felt a brief pang of guilt, knowing that she didn't often think about him. Yet she knew that, if he were back home, she wouldn't care how many strangers came to stay.

She made her entrance like an actress, a film star. She took possession.

They were all there, seated around the kitchen shelter-table. Cuffey, Adam, Abigail and Molly. Baby William was on Mrs Barnes' lap spooning food over his chin. And, sometimes, his mother's chin too.

It was a warm day and the kitchen door was open. She came round to the back and walked right in. Blue uniform, long legs, vivid dark lipstick, bobbed hair. She was every inch a performer. Cool and in command.

'My name is Pritt,' she said. 'P-r-i-double-t Pritt. *Hilda* Pritt.

'– I'm a pilot. First Officer Pritt, ectually.

'– Yes, young man, that's what I said! I fly for the ATA.

'– The Air Transport Auxiliary. That explains the uniform. I suppose you've never heard of us down here in the wilds of – God, where *is* this place? We ferry planes to and from airfields. From the factories where they're built. Fighters, mostly.

'– So I'm to have a room kept for me here. On standby. For whenever I bring a plane into your local airfield and need a bed for the night. Which will be quite orfen, ectually.

'– I know exactly what you're thinking. But a girl *can* fly planes. I've just brought in a brand-new Hurricane to your local airfield. All on my little own-io.'

'– There are nine of us. Women pilots, I mean. Have you heard of Amy Johnson? Well, she's one of us, ectually.

'– And about 150 men. Well, you would expect that, wouldn't you?

'– I've flown Hurricanes, Spitfires, Glosters, and Tiger Moths! *And* some German planes. When they've crash-landed or been captured, and needed to be taken to one of our bases.

'– So I flew them. Two Heinkels, and a Stuka. It's tricky work. If you don't take care, you end up with a tangle of scrap metal and a splat of raspberry jam all over the ground.

'– Got shot at once – by British ack-ack. Near Dover. Flying a Heinkel over from France. That was before Dunkirk. But can you believe it? – nobody had warned Defence! So they tried to bring me down. Men, of course. It's always men. The whole War is being run by men!

'– Still, they have their uses – if you want to be taken out for a drink. Golly, I really need a fag. Pass the ash-tray, Mr – what did you say your name was?

'– Scotland is the worst. Made a few trips to Scotland last winter. Jolly cold up there.

'– Did you say your name was Adam? I say, which

one of you two is Eve?

'– *What's* that you're doing? Rupert *Bear*! Gosh, what a joke! The world is falling apart all around us and you're reading Rupert Bear! When the Germans come bursting into your house, they'll find you pasting jolly old Rupert Bear into a scrap-book!

'– Lord! What's that ghastly *smell*?

'– Well, I suppose I'll survive. But, *please*, when I'm in my room, no interruptions from you three kids! Even if Adolf Hitler arrives at the door with the entire Gestapo and a couple of Panzer divisions, *don't come troubling me!*

'– Frankly, I would have preferred the Crown, where the American pilots stay. But the Ministry said No. I expect your place is cheaper. So here I am. Lucky old you!

'– Do you have a lounge?

'– You do? Jolly good! Well, toodle-oo then. Until supper.'

What American pilots? Adam wondered.

'I hate her!' Abigail declared later. 'We all hate her. *Don't* we?'

Molly nodded, tearfully. 'She was horrible to everyone. Even the baby!' She was indignant on behalf of her little brother. 'He couldn't help it if he made his nappy pong just at that moment!'

'*Adam!*'

'What?'

'We all hate Hilda Pritt, *don't* we?' Abigail said.

'She flies those planes,' he said slowly.

'So what? She's still a horrible person. She was nasty to everybody!'

Was that admiration in Adam's voice? Even envy perhaps? Molly watched him.

'In the middle of winter,' Adam said. 'Flying to Scotland. Up there, all alone in a cockpit. There's no heating in those planes. It would be several degrees below freezing. Trying to find her way with clouds and mountains all around her. Rain, snow sometimes, and in the dark perhaps.'

The two girls stared at him.

'No-one to tell her what to do, or how to do it. If she succeeds, fine. If she makes a mistake, the plane will hit a mountainside and she'll be dead.'

'I don't care. She's *still* a nasty person!'

'Up in the clouds there's no-one to be nasty to,' Adam said. 'It's just her.' He knew he wasn't making his meaning clear.

'So you *don't* think she's a nasty person?' demanded Abigail.

'It doesn't matter,' Adam said, still lost in thought.

But it mattered to Abigail. She was furious with Hilda Pritt.

After Sunday School, Molly went for a walk with Cuffey. He wanted to see the river, he said, in spite of the rain.

They stood on Silty Bridge and studied the Great Ouse, wide and slow, freckled with a billion vanishing rain-bubbles, comfortable and massive between its high grassy banks.

Molly remembered the day before her father left home to join the army. She and Abigail had been playing under the bridge where there was a cave-like place at the water's edge. They had crouched there in silence, not wanting to be seen. After a while, they had leaned cautiously out and looked up to see who was there. Mr Barnes could be seen, leaning on the rail and watching the river pass under him.

For what seemed like a long time, he had stood there, motionless. Then he walked away, back towards the town. They heard his steps above them, growing fainter as he left the bridge. He crossed the railway and they heard the first pedestrian's crossing-gate slam shut. Then the other one.

They'd given way to an outburst of giggles, Molly remembered. But there was no laughter in her now.

She wondered what her dad had been thinking the day before he left home.

'*Is* it oozy?' Cuffey asked.

'Its bottom is!' Molly said. 'We swim in it sometimes. In the summer.' In her head she made a joke. She would tell Abigail, and Abigail would say that Baby William had an oozy bottom. If Abigail didn't say it, Molly would. But it wasn't a joke she could share with Cuffey.

'Strange,' said Cuffey. 'Rivers usually run through the *lowest* part of the countryside. This one is *higher* than everything around it.'

Molly had never thought how strange it was. This was her river. All other rivers were to be judged by it.

'I suppose,' Cuffey said slowly, 'a few well-placed explosions on the river bank would flood the entire countryside.'

'Cuffey?' Molly said.

'Yes?'

'Do you think the Germans will invade us?'

Cuffey thought for a moment. 'No,' he said. 'Most people think they've left it too late and missed their chance. It's autumn now. The days are getting shorter and the weather is getting worse. They couldn't make the sea-crossing.'

Molly felt reassured. But Cuffey went on: 'They might try next spring, though. Around May.'

'All Germans are evil!' Molly said. 'I *hate* them!'

'Do you really think they are all evil?' Cuffey asked.

'Yes! They must be! Think of all the countries they've started wars with!'

The rain beat steadily on Cuffey's umbrella.

'Hmm. Imagine this. There are two make-believe countries. In one of them, all the people are multi-coloured. Some are green, some are blue, some are mauve. And they can change from one colour to a different one several times a day. Bad people are purple – all the time. Other people just turn purple occasionally.'

They turned to set off towards home. Molly did a cheerful little skip as they walked. 'And the other lot?'

'They are multi-coloured too. Only in their country the wicked colour is yellow.'

'What happens?'

'They quarrel and go to war.'

'Oh!' Molly said. That was not what she had hoped for.

'Do you think,' he said thoughtfully, 'that the very day that war was declared all the people in the first country turned purple?'

Molly saw that she had been trapped. 'Well,' she said, 'they could still have a war as long as all the people in the other country turned yellow.'

Then she realised she had trapped herself. She thumped Cuffey with her fists.

Monday 7th October ~ after school

Molly's mum led Molly into the unused dining-room and shut the door. Then she knelt on the floor in front of her, and held her shoulders firmly. 'I've got something sad to tell you,' she said.

Molly felt her blood rush away from her face. 'Dad?' she whispered.

Mum shook her head passionately. 'No. Not *our* dad. But Abigail's mum has had some bad news.'

'What?' said Molly, but she knew really what the bad news must be.

'Abigail's dad is missing, feared dead. I'm afraid it means he's probably been killed.'

Molly stared, absorbing this.

'He was not one of the ones who got away at Dunkirk. And he's not in the lists of prisoners-of-war. So it means he's probably dead.'

'Just lying on the ground somewhere,' Molly whispered. With the rain falling on him, she thought.

Molly was worried that she didn't know how a best friend should behave in a situation like this. She wanted to be a good enough best friend for Abigail. But what should she do? What was she supposed to say? Abigail would be very sad and she would need some careful looking after, Molly thought.

But Abigail was not sad. If anything, she was brighter and dafter than she usually was. She said funnier things, and was cheekier in school – a new brassy Abigail who played crazy games while Molly dutifully followed along in her wake, wondering if Abigail would ever need her best friend.

Saturday 12th October

Adam helped the girls with their shopping on Saturday morning. They were leaving the butcher's shop when Adam stopped, listening.

Then Molly and Abigail heard it – a big aircraft, descending steadily as it approached the town.

'American,' he said. 'A Liberator.'

The girls looked at him in surprise. 'The Americans aren't in the War,' Abigail said.

Adam shrugged. He knew that perfectly well.

'They're on our side though,' Molly said. She liked to reassure herself.

It was to take Adam until Monday to find out about it. He was already an unofficial member of the aeroplane experts in his new class at school, and he found out that there were regular flights from the USA. It was Marion Staines who eventually told him; her grandfather owned the Crown. There were two flights every week between Washington and a local airfield; she knew because some of the flight crews stayed at her granddad's hotel.

On Saturday afternoon, Abigail came round and said she wanted to go to Paradise Barn. 'Like we used to,' she said. 'Just the two of us. And take a picnic.'

This idea appealed to Molly too. They both loved Paradise Barn. It was a couple of fields away from Molly's home and they had played there ever since they were about six or seven. It was a huge old brick building, with a pair of massive doors. It belonged to Mr Morton and was used for storing old farm machinery. He had caught them there once, years ago. He had walked straight in and found them playing pirates on one of his ancient tractors. They stared at him; he stared at them. Then he had given them each a toffee, told them not to mess about with the farm machinery, and walked out.

So they knew they were allowed.

They took two kitkats, two apples, two hard-boiled eggs and a bottle of ginger beer, and set off for the Barn.

All afternoon, Molly kept a wary eye on Abigail. But everything seemed all right – until Abigail announced that she was going to climb the big tree. It was an enormous oak tree, and it grew close to the barn, dwarfing the huge old building.

They always climbed it slowly, together, and stopped when they got to what they called the big V-branch. But not this time. Abigail raced up through the branches as if a demon were pursuing her, and Molly couldn't keep up. 'Come *on!*' Abigail shouted.

'Why are you going so high?' Molly asked, breathless and a bit scared.

'There might be a clue up here.'

'Clue? What sort of clue?'

'A clue to the murder, of course! It's time we found out who did it.'

Molly considered. 'You really think the murderer might have put a clue at the top of a tree?' She was not being sarcastic. She was confused and anxious.

But Abigail was possessed. She seemed to have set caution aside and she was heading out along the huge V-branch. Molly knew she couldn't follow her and, when Abigail fell unaccountably silent, Molly climbed back down to the ground. She stood there, worried and cross, looking up.

Abigail clambered out so far that she was above the roof of the Barn. Coolly, she stepped from the tree to the roof, stood boldly upright, and did a little curtsey. Then, more abruptly than she had meant to, she sat down on the uneven red tiles.

Slowly she slid down the roof, trying to get a hold. The branch was now out of her reach, above her head. The tiles were mossy and rough, and she stopped slipping at the bottom, with her heels dug into the rain gutter.

'Your knickers!' Molly shouted up. 'You get into terrible trouble when you muck up your knickers.'

But Abigail was not concerned about her knickers. Her reckless courage had evaporated and she was too scared to speak. She sat, paralysed, on the edge of the roof, staring down at Molly.

So this is what a best friend has to do, Molly thought crossly. I have to find a way of getting Abigail down!

She raced round into the barn, where she knew there was an ancient wooden ladder hanging from two great nails high in the wall. She and Abigail had climbed up a few rungs once. Molly hurried over to it. She managed to wriggle it about until the top rung came free of the nails. Luckily it fell slowly, so that Molly could jump out of the way. She stood back, aghast, as the ladder fell with a great dusty crash onto the brick floor of the barn.

Some alert part of her mind registered that there was something different about those bricks. But there was no time for such thoughts and she hurried to the end of the ladder to drag it outside. But she knew at once that this was impossible. She could – just – lift one end off the ground, and even drag the whole thing a yard or two. But she knew that she would never be able on her own to raise it against the wall where Abigail was.

Molly despaired then. She let the ladder fall to the ground again, and raced outside. Abigail had not moved. She was still on the edge of the roof, held by her heels stuck into the rain gutter.

Molly looked around her. Across the fields, about a quarter of a mile away, Cuffey was walking towards the town . She screamed at him. '*Cuffey! Cuffey!*'

She saw him stop and look round. Then he saw her

and began hurrying along the footpath towards Paradise Barn. As he approached, he took in what had happened. Molly was crying, relieved that help had arrived, but angry because she wasn't strong enough to lift the ladder herself.

Cuffey pulled the ladder outside and round to where Abigail was. He raised it, with difficulty, against the wall and climbed slowly to the top. He seemed to have no fear of heights. Molly watched from the ground as he reached the top and stood beside Abigail.

He was there for ages, quietly talking to the petrified girl. She was unable to move a muscle. She sat there, white-faced and scared, with her heels dug in and her hands struggling for a grip on the tiles. But at last he persuaded her that she could shift around and onto the ladder. He directed every move, quietly telling her to do this with her left foot, to do that with her right hand, to shift her weight onto her knees, and so on.

Eventually, Abigail stood on the ladder, at the top, safely contained in Cuffey's arms, and they began to move slowly down together.

But there was no time for relief. As Abigail and Cuffey reached the ground, the air-raid siren began to wail. That whining up-and-down sound always made Molly feel sick. She realised that for some minutes she had been dimly aware of the sound of approaching planes.

'*Come on!*' Cuffey shouted. 'We have to find a shelter!'

When there was an air-raid, the rule was that you went to the nearest house, but Molly knew that the nearest houses did not have proper shelters. The nearest one with a shelter was her own. So they hurried home, Molly holding Abigail's hand and almost dragging her along. Cuffey, breathless now, followed behind at a distance.

As they tore up to Molly's back door, eight Stukas roared overhead, not far above their rooftops, their crew intent upon killing. They could see the pilots' heads, in tight leather helmets. One of them looked down directly at Molly. Higher flew a squadron of Messerschmitts.

Molly's Mum stood anxiously inside the back door. 'Into the shelter! Quick!' she said.

One of the sides was open, and Adam was already in there, crouching in the shadows. He kept a spare pad and some pencils in the shelter. They were no use at night but during daylight raids he could draw. He glanced up at Molly as she crawled in, and gave her a quick cordial smile.

Abigail never got to the shelter. She fell into Molly's Mum's arms and cried and cried as if her head were full of water.

Then Cuffey arrived and stood in the doorway, breathless. With a free hand, Mum waved to him to get into the shelter. From there, appalled and frightened, Molly watched her friend weeping uncontrollably as if the whole world were coming to an end.

Mum was still kneeling on the kitchen floor, holding Abigail tight and talking quietly to her, when the all-clear sounded.

I wasn't needed after all, Molly thought.

Molly awoke in the middle of the night thinking about Paradise Barn. Its floor – or, to be more precise, the bricks which the floor was made of.

They were ancient floor-bricks, grimy yellow, and with a slight shine on the surface, worn and scuffed. But, when she had gone in search of the ladder, there had been a difference. Now, in the middle of the night, Molly remembered what the difference was.

In one part of the floor, some of the bricks had changed. The whole floor of the barn was littered with dirt, old leaves blown in from last autumn, wisps of straw. But the bricks in that small patch were different: they were slightly uneven, and some had a rough and gritty surface.

She resolved to tell Abigail about it first thing in the morning. At that moment, the siren sounded and Molly got up and went downstairs to join Adam and the two lodgers in the shelter.

Wednesday 16th October

All that week Molly and Adam went to school through the town. There was no point in going to Abigail's house because Abigail wasn't there. She and her mother had gone to Sheffield to visit Abigail's grandmother. An elderly signalman from Ely had been brought out of retirement to stay in the railway house and open and close the crossing-gates until they came back.

Without Abigail, Molly was restless and bad-tempered. She spent a lot of time with Adam but he didn't make up for Abigail. On Wednesday morning there was a postcard: 'We're coming home on Saturday. Meet us at the station at 4.15.' This cheered her.

'I'm going to London after school,' Adam said. 'On the 3.45.'

Before she had time to be amazed, Adam went on. 'I've got enough money for two tickets. We can get the 8 o'clock train back from Liverpool Street.'

We? Go to London without a grown-up? Without telling anyone? It was impossible! Didn't he know there was a War on? But she knew she would never have dared even if there had been no War.

'Why?' She heard the word come gasping out of

her as if she were out of breath.

'I want to get my books before the Jerries bomb them to smithereens.'

'But you can't just . . . And, anyway, what will my mum say?'

'Your mum isn't going to be home at all this afternoon. She said so. And she's going out this evening.'

This was true. Mum had promised to help Mrs Weathergreen to whitewash her outside toilet. Baby William was going with her. She would have tea there and then she was going to Littleport on the bus to visit Auntie Phyllis. Molly's aunt was a bus conductress six days a week but Wednesday was her day off.

'Your mum's leaving cold meals for everyone. We'll be back before she gets in.'

'But . . . ' Molly was full of *buts*. This was impossible! She knew it was impossible. But how do you say no to someone who makes decisions just like that?

Molly did the next best thing. 'If *you* want to go, Adam Swales, I can't stop you. But don't expect me to go with you!'

I sound like Abigail's mum, she thought.

Adam said nothing. He wasn't angry; he didn't seem to be disappointed; and he didn't try to persuade her. He just got on with going to school.

Prayers, arithmetic, drill, playtime, English, dinnertime, drawing and – finally! – the afternoon story. And all the time a kind of half-decision grew like mischief in Molly's head.

The train was at 3.45. At 3.30 Adam hurried out of school and ran all the way to Great Deeping station. He bought a half-return to Liverpool Street, and crossed the tracks to the up platform. No-one else was there. He leaned back on the railings and watched the road from the town.

There seemed to be no movement in the soft October afternoon. Inside the station building someone was playing Glen Miller's *In the Mood*. When it stopped, there was silence. A bell clanged in the signal-box at the end of the platform.

Adam saw Molly in the distance, running towards the station. She's fast, he thought. He walked unhurriedly back across the tracks to the ticket office and bought another ticket. When he came out of the office, Molly reached the top of the steps and stood there clutching her side.

'Stitch!' she gasped. 'Cuffey's going to be out tonight. I remembered. I didn't want to spend the evening with Hilda Pritt!'

She might have saved her breath. Adam wasn't interested in explanations. He grabbed her arm and led her along the platform, down the slope and across the tracks to the other side. The train was already steaming round the bend towards them.

There was a prolonged blast of steam, a slamming of doors, a whistle, and a hoot from the engine. Molly Barnes was on her way to London.

Adam led Molly out of Liverpool Street station – under a different sky, *his* sky. The train had arrived late and they had only an hour to walk to his house, find the books he wanted, and return to the station in time to catch the last train back.

Molly had a new thought – something else to worry about. 'Will your parents be there?'

Adam doubted it. His mother worked late on most days, and his father practically lived at the fire station because of the blitz.

London was making itself ready for another night of bombing. Molly moved through the strangeness of it all like a traveller in the underworld. They entered a street where there was an eerie silence. It was closed to traffic. A double-decker tram lay flat across the road on its side, blocking the way, with its wheels exposed to view. Under it, there was a huge hole with the buckled tram-lines linking one side to the other like metallic skipping-ropes. A policeman stood guard.

'I'm hungry,' Molly said. 'Can we buy something to eat? I've got a shilling.'

Adam nodded. 'Over there,' he said.

Molly would not have known it was a shop. It had no windows, just wooden boards; and no light was showing.

She hadn't the courage to go in. 'You go,' she said. It would be like going into a hole.

They crossed the road. A dog cocked its leg against the roof of the fallen tram. Molly followed Adam into the shop. The darkness was impenetrable at first, but an old man was somehow managing to count his day's takings. He sold them two bread rolls, with some jam. *Bread-bombs*, he called them.

The next street was noisier, full of people and traffic. On the left, the houses seemed intact. Their doors – with house-numbers and letter-boxes and door-knockers – suggested normality and the regular doings of daily life. But this was an illusion: they were empty shells, with no roofs, no glass in the windows. Some still had curtains, moving dismally in the evening air. The night sky still held some remaining light, and it shone through the empty glassless windows in a baleful way, as if in a horror film. On the right, there were no buildings at all – just piles of bricks and plaster, and great smashed beams of wood.

There was no footpath. The fallen rubble had been cleared from the middle of the road and left in long uneven piles along the edges.

Adam led her into a different street. Molly saw a wall left high and dry. Lofty it was, towering above them, with all its different wall-papers exposed. Some of them were torn and blowing loosely in the air. A brick chimney-stack went from the ground right to the top, with a fireplace at every level, big ones at the bottom, smaller ones higher up. And mantle-pieces where people had stood their clocks, or vases, or china knick-knacks. A wash-basin still clung to the highest part of the wall and a small mirror still hung on its hook, slightly crooked, catching the last faint gleam of daylight.

Someone nearby had a wireless on, or perhaps a gramophone, and a cheerful voice was singing along with Tommy Dorsey's *I'll Never Smile Again*.

Molly looked longingly up at the sky. There was a single plane up there, too high to identify, turning to the west in an immense curve, silver in the last of the daylight.

Adam looked up. 'American,' he said. 'From Northolt, probably.' Molly had never heard of Northolt, but her heart went out to the solitary aircraft flying up and away into the distant west.

When they got to Adam's street, they found it had been blocked off. An ARP man shoved back his tin helmet, wiped his forehead, and told them there was an unexploded bomb near the front door of number three. Until it had been safely cleared away, this end of the street was closed and all the houses had been evacuated.

They could get to the other end of the street by going round the block. Molly was worrying again. It was all taking so long.

In the darkness, Adam's house seemed small to Molly. It was one of a long high terrace of buildings, all with their front doors opening onto the street. While he was feeling under the doorstep for the key, an old man came out of the next-door house. He wanted to chat with Adam, and Molly began to fidget inwardly with the need to get on.

'I suppose my mum and dad aren't at home?' Adam said.

The old man shook his head. 'Don't see much of your mum these days. She spends all her nights at work. Apparently there's a good air-raid shelter at her office. And your dad – well, he practically lives at the fire station these days.'

Adam unlocked his front door.

'I've been feeding your Tibby,' the old man said. 'She's got a taste for corned beef. Took some right off the end of my fork yesterday! Stuck out one paw and just took it! Laugh? You should've heard my wife! I thought she was going to peg out!'

Inside there was absolute darkness. And an unexpected silence. Adam took Molly's arm and led her through the hall and into the kitchen at the back. Already Molly sensed that the house was larger than it seemed from outside. The rooms were long and the ceilings high. Outside she could dimly see a small backyard, just big enough for a dustbin.

Adam felt in the usual place for a torch. He switched it on, taking care not to direct it towards any of the windows. 'I won't put the lights on,' he said. 'We haven't time to close the shutters.'

He led her upstairs, to the first floor, and then to the floor above. In the light of the torch, Molly saw a grey-and-white cat following them. 'Tibby,' she whispered to it.

There was a shout from the street below them. 'The bastards!'

Molly and Adam stopped. The sound of approaching planes could be heard. There had been no air-raid warning this time. Something had gone wrong. The noise – a low menacing roar with a soft under-whisper – was growing rapidly louder. They pressed their faces to the nearest window and peered upwards.

The darkening sky was filled with Nazi aircraft, hundreds of them it seemed, flying high and steady. Molly had never imagined there were so many aircraft in the whole world. The noise was beyond belief; you could *hear* the weight of the thousands of tons of bombs they had inside them.

Adam dashed into his room and came out almost at once with his books – three big books about art. At that moment, the air-raid warning sounded, almost obliterated by the thunder of the planes overhead.

There were heavy thudding sounds from far away, swift whining screams, and great crashes from close at hand. The non-stop thunder of explosions. Lights flashed and a nearby building fell like an avalanche. The noise was deafening. Molly felt the house rocking like a ship at sea.

The cat jumped from a windowsill and miaowed angrily. They were on their way down from the top of the stairs. There was a flash of dazzling light from the street outside. It was like a dream – for a fraction of a second all the glass from the windows bubbled inwards, then flew horizontally into the wall opposite before crumbling to the floor in fragments. If they had been by one of the windows, they would have been cut to bits. A blast of air slammed them sideways and for a brief moment the breath was sucked out of their lungs.

The cat hissed.

Then, as if in a soundless nightmare, Molly saw that the outside wall was not there. Slowly she understood that the stairs they were standing on – which had once been inside the house – was now on the outside. Below them, on their right, was the open night and the street below, with people fleeing from the falling masonry. One or two faces were looking up at them. There was no roof above their heads, just some bare rafters between them and the enemy-occupied sky. Roof-tiles were pouring down into the street.

Molly thought she had been deafened for life. She stooped to pick up the cat. Tibby pressed back her ears, hissed, and sank her claws and teeth into Molly's sleeve. But Molly knew about cats. She raced into the bathroom, grabbed a towel and wrapped it tightly round the terrified animal so that only its angry head was visible.

Adam was shouting at her. 'Come *on*!' His voice came to her faintly, as if from a long way off. But his face was only a few inches away from hers. His hair and face were covered with fine grey dust – his eyebrows and lashes too.

They stumbled down the stairs. As they went, part of the roof disintegrated and fell into the street. The house seemed to be melting around them. A lump of concrete landed on the stairs above them and bounced down the wooden steps, overtaking them, before it fell sideways into the street. There were people down there who had seen them. They were looking up and shouting.

In the hall, they found that the door-frame had shifted slightly so that the front door was jammed.

'The back door!' Adam shouted. But they couldn't get to it. The kitchen was under an enormous heap of rubble, with dust milling around like smoke. Under it, was Adam's shelter-table.

They raced back to the front door. Someone out in the street was banging and thumping at it, and in a moment the door was smashed open. Adam and Molly rushed out into the street into the arms of a policeman.

'Is there anyone else in there?'

'No! Only us!'

'You sure?'

The policeman made them scramble over the piles of rubble, keeping to the middle of the street because slates were slicing down from neighbouring buildings. Fat billows of smoke streamed slowly overhead, lit from underneath by burning buildings. The fire brigade had somehow already managed to get there, and two firemen stood, gazing upwards, directing a massive stream of water at the burning roof-rafters of a nearby building.

Molly had stopped being aware of sounds. But there were smells – the smell of explosives, escaping gas, brick-dust.

She saw a young woman clutching an old clock. She shouted something at Molly and Adam. Adam's elderly neighbour appeared from somewhere with an aspidistra in a brass coal-scuttle. The stately leaves of the aspidistra bounced and shivered indignantly at such an outrage.

'Shouldn't we try to get to a shelter?' Molly said. She knew she sounded feeble. She had no idea where the shelters were, what they looked like, or whether strangers were allowed. She had a hazy picture in her head of knocking at a shelter door and politely saying 'May I come in, please?'

'It will be quicker to go to the station,' the policeman said. And for just a few cheering moments Molly thought he meant the railway station. Perhaps they could still get their train.

But he took them to a police station and showed them into a cell with a thick metal door. Molly was truly terrified. Was she going to be locked up?

'Now, you both get under one of those benches. Believe me, this is one of the best air-raid shelters in London. We don't like Hitler to get at our villains!'

The bombing went on for two hours. Then there was a lull, and a different policeman brought them drinks of water and some cheese sandwiches.

Molly's hearing had come back, but there seemed to be a non-stop roaring inside her ears.

Through all that, Adam had kept a firm grip on his three books. Eagerly he searched through one of them until he found what he wanted. 'There!' he said. 'That's the one!'

Molly was mystified. 'The painting that was stolen in Paris,' Adam said impatiently.

Molly recognised it eventually. Dimly it came back to her from an older innocent world. *Vue de Pointeuse* by Camille Pissarro. Did Adam *never* stop thinking about art? Had he been thinking about this painting all the time, even when they were almost blown to bits?

She still held the cat.

Sitting on the bench in the prison cell, she gave herself up to misery. She had no idea of the time, but she knew there was now no way out of the mess she had got herself into.

They were questioned as soon as the first wave of bombs had passed. Who were they, where did they come from, why were they here? No-one was angry with them, no-one spoke sharply to them. But someone went off to phone Great Deeping two-nine. Mrs Barnes must be told where they were.

Sitting miserably on the bench, Molly decided to unwrap the poor cat. Tibby had long ago stopped hissing and swearing, but her ears were still laid back and she glared angrily at Molly. Adam watched as Molly carefully pulled away the bloody towel.

The cat's left foreleg was not there. It had been cut away entirely. That flying glass on the stairs, Molly thought. The stump could not be seen, but blood still oozed from somewhere in the filthy tangled fur. Molly saw Adam turn white. He swayed and fell against her shoulder.

Molly wrapped the towel around the cat, more carefully this time to reduce the bleeding. Then she turned to Adam, gently leaning him back against the wall. The policeman had stood a glass of water on the bench beside her. She dipped her finger into it and shook a couple of drops onto Adam's cheek. It didn't work – so she poured the whole lot over him.

The train they should have caught did not leave Liverpool Street. Near Clapton, a bomb hit a railway bridge and destroyed the track.

Thursday 17th October

In the morning Tom Swales turned up, Adam's dad.

'You must be Molly,' he said to her. 'I hope he's been behaving himself – down in the country.'

Molly just gaped. The world was in ruins! Did he expect her to chat politely about Adam's behaviour?

The duty policeman had arranged a big fried breakfast but Molly hadn't been able to eat any of it. All the time, she felt as if she was going to be sick.

Adam and his dad wanted to see the wreckage of their home. Molly didn't want to go with them. One of the policemen had phoned home, and what would happen if her mum came for her and she wasn't there? But neither did she want to stay at the police station by herself.

So she went with them, feeling wretched and forgotten. It was raining drearily from low clouds. The smell of smoke and wet brick-dust was everywhere. In the street where Adam's house had been, a bulldozer was already clearing the middle of the road, dumping the débris in mountainous piles along the edges. A few people were about, climbing over the rubble in search of anything they could salvage from their homes. One end of the street was untouched by the bombing; the other end had been obliterated. Adam's house and two or three each side of it had disappeared completely, except parts of the back wall.

There was an ambulance and two uniformed women were carrying a stretcher, covered with a sheet. Molly stared, realising slowly what she was seeing. The thought came into her head of the poor man who had been murdered at Great Deeping. His body, too, had been lying all night in the rain. The thought of him seemed to be in hiding, ready to trouble her at any moment.

She thought longingly of Abigail – lovely loyal Abigail, with her slightly elfin eyes and wide lopsided mouth that could smile so broadly.

'Is Mum coming?' Adam said to his father.

'No, Adam, she's not. There's something . . . '

In spite of her own misery, Molly knew at once that there was a carefulness about the way Mr Swales spoke.

'Adam, I have something to tell you.'

They were standing, all three, at the place where until last night Adam's front door-step had been. It was probably still there, buried under the fallen masonry.

Molly had a sudden thought, a sharp tiny curiosity which went through her before time could catch up with it. Whatever this news was going to be, would Adam be able to *draw* it?

'You know she's been working in an office at the

War Department? Well, she's not any more.'

There was a puzzled frown on Mr Swales' face. 'She's been and joined the WAAFs,' he said.

'The Women's Auxiliary Air Force?'

Mr Swales nodded. 'Yep, that's just what she's done! She's away doing her training right now.' Then he shook his head, mystified, and turned to Molly. 'She sometimes does that sort of thing – impulsive, you know. Takes your breath away sometimes.'

So *that's* where he gets it from, Molly thought.

Mr Swales sighed. 'I suppose this won't matter much,' he said, indicating the ruined remains of their home. '*She* won't be living in London any more, *I* can stay at your grandmother's, and *you're* living out in the country anyway. I expect we'll make a fresh start when the War's over. Like everyone else.'

Adam, quietly approving, was imagining his mother in uniform.

When they got back to the police station, a familiar figure was standing in the street outside, under a big black umbrella.

'*Cuffey!*'

Molly tore down the street and threw herself into his arms. He held her firmly in his big embrace. 'I've come to take you home,' he said.

Molly felt a prickling of tears at the back of her eyes and knew that once she started to cry there would be a flood. But Cuffey forestalled it. 'I suppose we have to take that other evacuee with us?' he asked.

'What other evacuee?'

'The three-legged one.'

Bit by bit, she learned what had happened. Cuffey told the story so clearly that she could see almost every detail – how her mother had been dismayed when she came home to find Molly and Adam were not there; how dismay had turned into fear when the police phoned from London; and how this had given way to panic when they insisted that someone had to fetch them.

The problem was Baby William. Molly understood that at once. Mrs Barnes absolutely would not take him to London in the middle of the blitz. It was a hell-hole there, Mrs Barnes thought, and Molly thought so too. But William was unwell, with a fever and a high temperature. Just a minor baby's ailment probably – but there was no-one she was prepared to leave him with while she went up to London herself. Perhaps Hilda Pritt might be persuaded . . .

' – Oh, I say! No, I jolly well will *not*! I'm your lodger, Mrs Burns, not your children's nanny.

' – Yes, I know how trying it is for you! But it's out of the question! I'm *sorry*! It's one thing to face enemy planes when I'm up in the air with them, but I'll be blowed if I'm going to let them drop bombs on me while I'm scuttling about on the ground like a . . . like a bloomin' rabbit!

' – I think you should try to calm down, dear. Getting

hysterical isn't going to help. The two wretched children were perfectly able to go orff to London on their own, so there's no bally reason why they shouldn't come home the same way.'

' – Now *is* there?'

Mrs Barnes was at her wits' end. Then Cuffey said, 'I'll fetch them.'

There was just time for Cuffey to catch the last train to Liverpool Street. It left on time, but – because of the bomb at Clapton – it had to be diverted through Seven Sisters. There was bomb damage on that line too, and it took the train all night to make its dreary and dangerous way into Liverpool Street station.

Shortly after dawn, Cuffey had walked out into the rain in poor bomb-weary London.

'Mum?'

'What is it, Molly?'

'When are you going to . . . ?'

'What?'

Hesitation. Should she say it? '*Punish* me?'

'I'm not going to punish you, Molly. Cuffey says that what happened in London was sufficient punishment for a lifetime.'

Molly felt tears coming.

'But I *have* got something to say.'

'What?' Molly wondered why her voice came out as a whisper. She was still half-deafened.

'That was a very bad thing you did, Molly. *Very very* bad. I couldn't believe it!'

'I know.' The tears were pressing harder.

'I have said what needed to be said to Adam. He said he was sorry. I was surprised because I didn't think he ever apologized for anything – but he did. He said you were not to blame because he persuaded you to go with him.'

They were running down Molly's face now, the tears.

'Now, Molly, listen to me. I am sure it was his idea. And I'm sure he *did* persuade you to go with him. But, Molly love, if someone persuades you to do a bad thing, *it is still your responsibility if you say yes*. Do you understand me?'

Molly nodded passionately. She wiped her sleeve across her wet and snuffly face.

'Come here then,' Mum said. There was a close confusion of hair and wet cheeks, and from somewhere inside it Molly heard Mum's stifled voice say: '*You might have been killed!*'

Molly didn't think about God very much. But it occurred to her that she ought to send Him a thankyou prayer. So, on Saturday afternoon, when she set out to meet Abigail at the station, she left early and called in at the church.

She was familiar with the church. She went there every week for Sunday School. It was *hers*, sturdy and unchanging, with its stumpy tower snuggling among ancient trees.

There was a small pile of sand in the porch, and a bucket and a bag of cement. But there was no-one inside – if there had been she wouldn't have gone in. She said her thank-you prayer and sat back for a moment or two in the pew.

A special mood came over her, private and familiar. This happened sometimes and she had never told anyone about it, not even Abigail. This was *her* church, in *her* town, where her house was, and where her friends lived. And the great flat farmlands around it were her Garden of Eden. The feeling made her shiver.

In her head, Molly decided to make up a poem. I'll call it *Eden in England*, she thought.

Through the yellowy glass windows she could see leaves falling gently down to settle on the graves in the churchyard. Molly watched them, distracted and absorbed. Her poem got no further than its title.

Did they have autumn in Eden?

One of the stained-glass windows in the south wall showed Adam and Eve, with the serpent. Molly was a Sunday School girl and she knew all about Adam and Eve. They were naked, standing under the Tree of Knowledge. Adam was gazing at Eve, and Eve was looking up at the fruit hanging on the tree. But the serpent, which was winding itself up between them, looked out of the picture with a lurid green eye. Adam and Eve were safely part of an old, old story – but the serpent seemed to be saying to anyone who looked at it 'I am part of *you*!'

When she was little, Molly used to have nightmares about that serpent – richly coloured in red and green and purple, its mouth open wide in a wicked, wicked grin. It still troubled her at times, that grin with its sharp curved teeth – and now the thought came to her that there was a serpent in *her* Garden of Eden too. A wickedness which had changed things, a killer who had struck in the night and left a man lying dead in the rain.

Somewhere there was someone who secretly knew. Someone with an evil knowing eye like the serpent's, and a wicked, wicked grin.

The colours of the window were projected by the sun onto Molly's hands as they lay crossed in her lap.

She moved them and watched as the reds and purples and greens slid over her wrists and along her fingers. Their outlines were blurred but the colours were vivid and rich.

She became aware of noises outside the church door and decided to leave. In the porch she found Mr Rennie the verger.

'Careful you don't step on my wet cement, Molly Barnes,' he said.

Some of the old floor-bricks had become cracked and loose. Mr Rennie had taken them out and was filling and smoothing the gaps with fresh mortar.

'Whole building's falling to bits,' he grumbled. 'Won't be nothing left in fifty years! Still, I won't be here either, so it won't make no difference to me.'

'When the War's over . . . ' Molly was going to say something cheerful about how things would get better again one day. Everybody did that. It was a favourite expression: *When the War's over . . .*

But Mr Rennie wasn't listening. 'I shan't ever get to ring those bells no more, neither,' he said sadly. He knelt up from his handiwork and pushed his cap back from his brow.

There had been no ringing for a year now. Except once, on September 7th, to warn everyone that the German army was coming. Operation Cromwell, it had been called. They hadn't invaded, it had been a false alarm. But Molly would never forget that damp grey summer evening a few weeks ago. Everyone for miles around had heard the bells. Molly remembered her mum; she had straightened up from her work, put her arm tightly round Molly, and sighed deeply.

Molly stepped carefully around the cemented patch. Out onto the High Street she went, thinking about floor-bricks. I've *still* not told Abigail about those floor-bricks in Paradise Barn, she thought.

But as she raced past the Crown Hotel, she got distracted. The big front doors were open and inside stood Cuffey, talking to a stranger. Molly stopped and stared in. Cuffey? In the Crown?

Cuffey saw her outside and came down the wide steps to greet her. Her dismay must have shown on her face, for he said at once, 'Molly! What is it?'

Molly didn't mince her words. 'Are you going to move into the Crown?' she said. 'Don't you like our guesthouse any more?'

Understanding dawned on Cuffey. 'Molly, I love being at your mother's guesthouse. As long as my visit to Great Deeping lasts, that's where I will stay. I promise.'

'Then why . . . ?'

'I came here on business,' he said. 'Now, enough! I've promised – and I don't break promises.'

With an explosion of happiness and energy, Molly tore along Station Road, eager to see Abigail again and restore things fully to the way they should be.

All Saturday morning, while Molly was doing her mother's shopping, Adam had tried to draw. He sat at the kitchen table with his sketch-book and his pencils. He stopped for a while when they had dinner. Then he began again, and he was still there when Molly set off to the church. He didn't mind that Mrs Barnes was going about her work in and out of the kitchen, and making the usual sounds of housework. In fact, he liked it – as long as she didn't talk to him.

Mrs Barnes had the wireless on, and a man with a quavering voice was singing *It's a Lovely Day Tomorrow*.

For the first time ever, Adam couldn't draw what he wanted. He had intended to make a picture of the night sky over London, full of planes. He could see it in his mind – a great multitude of bombers, moving across the city in a huge sky-wide layer. They were so thick that – if it had been day-time – they would have shut out the sunlight.

But he couldn't get it right, and page after page was screwed up and thrown away. He was baffled. He had never had any difficulty before. His drawing had always been effortless and untroubled, clear fine lines and controlled sketching joyously appearing on the page.

Today, however, nothing would come without struggle and frustration. He tried drawing something else – his street in London with sticks of bombs swaying and wobbling down from the sky. The moment fractionally before the first of them hit the building, *that* was what he thought he wanted. The very last fraction of a moment in time when the house was still a house.

But that didn't work either. He disliked the feel of his hands. They were grubby, and his fingers felt sweaty and clumsy.

Then, much later and after many more attempts, his pencil found a purpose. To Adam, it felt as if the image had been hiding somewhere.

Mrs Barnes, moving about the kitchen and looking occasionally over his shoulder as she passed him, saw Molly appearing on the paper.

It was unmistakably Molly. She was sitting on a bench, seen from above and in front. Her hair had fallen forward over her eyes and there was her parting, a bit uneven, on the top of her head. On her lap was the cat, crouching and tense, ugly with fear and pain. Molly had her hands raised like someone surrendering, as if a gun was being pointed at her. She was looking down at the cat and – although her face could not be seen – everything in the drawing showed her dismay and pity.

Adam threw down his pencil and leaned back in his chair. Mrs Barnes sat on the chair next to him and together they looked at the drawing.

Mrs Barnes thought to herself: Molly *does* put up her hands like that – and I've never noticed before!

Adam was thinking: But I didn't see her from in front like that. I was *beside* her on the bench.

'Adam!' Mrs Barnes whispered. 'Oh, Adam!'

'Mrs Murfitt?'

Molly thought she was being very cunning in the wheedling way she used her voice. They were walking back from the station, she and Abigail sharing one of the cases behind Abigail's mum, who had the other one.

Mrs Murfitt was suspicious immediately. 'What?' she said, in the manner of a woman who did not intend to be outsmarted.

'You know you grumble a lot about the mice eating your garden seeds,' Molly said.

'Yeeess?' Abigail's mum said slowly.

'If you had a cat . . . '

'Well, I haven't!' said Mrs Murfitt.

'I know a cat you could have. It's from London and it's been bombed out.'

'You don't say!' Mrs Murfitt said.

'It's had one of its legs blown off,' Molly said. She thought this was a clincher. Who could refuse a home to one of Hitler's war victims?

'As far as I know,' Abigail's mum said slowly, 'the mice in my garden all have four legs. Which would give them an advantage over a cat with only three. So I'd prefer to have a cat with all its limbs complete, *if* you don't mind.'

Abigail and Molly exchanged grimaces.

Molly had so many things to tell Abigail that she completely forgot – again! – about the floor-bricks.

Monday 21st October ~ half-term holiday

Molly and Abigail were walking past the tiny house where Mrs Weathergreen lived. She was in her garden, and she came out into the road to speak to them.

'Abigail,' she said, 'I was so sorry to hear about your father.'

Abigail stared.

'You will find the strength that you need,' Mrs Weathergreen said.

'He might be all right – somewhere,' Abigail said. She was almost inaudible.

Molly saw Mrs Weathergreen hesitate, giving herself time to consider. Then she said, 'Abigail, I worked with the Red Cross in the last War. Their prisoner-of-war lists were very accurate.'

Abigail stood like a statue. 'Have you found your flower-press?' Molly asked Mrs Weathergreen.

The old lady sighed. 'No,' she said. 'I suppose *you* haven't heard anything about it?'

They shook their heads.

'If you do hear anything . . . you know . . . if any of the other children might have . . . taken it away . . . '

Molly noticed that there were tears in Mrs Weathergreen's eyes.

'Was it very special?' Abigail managed to ask. But her voice sounded sharp.

'Yes. My husband made it for me. He was very good at that kind of thing. You see, when we were first married, I had a sadness of my own. And he made the flower-press for me. It was *lovely!*'

'Wasn't it rather big for carrying around the countryside?'

'Oh, yes, far too big! I had an ordinary small one when I went collecting. Then, when I got home in the evenings, I would sit at the table and arrange all my finds in the big flower-press. He would play the piano. We were very happy.'

Molly watched. Yes, she thought to herself, despite all the dead people in the War, Mrs Weathergreen is allowed to be sad about her flower-press.

'When did you last see it?' Molly asked.

Mrs Weathergreen smiled. 'You sound exactly like the policeman who came to see me about it,' she said. 'You remember some time ago – in September – I had an exhibition of pressed wild flowers in the church hall? It was on that dreadful Saturday – when the bells rang and we all thought the Germans were going to invade us. Well, I had it there. I put it in the little outside toilet, and when I went to get it, well . . .'

'It had gone?'

'Someone said they'd seen it in the long grass over by

the hedge, but I went to look there the next day . . . and someone had . . . it wasn't there.'

She can't bring herself to say *stolen*, Molly realised. She doesn't want to think the world is so wicked.

'Abigail,' Mrs Weathergreen said, 'I have something for you. I've been waiting for a chance to give it to you.'

She hurried inside and returned with a small flat package. Abigail's name was written on it.

Abigail stood a little stupidly, looking at the package in her hand. Molly nudged her with her shoulder, and she opened it and took out a small silver photograph frame, with no picture in it.

'Have you any pictures of your father?' Mrs Weathergreen said.

Abigail nodded dumbly.

'You might find that you won't want to look at them for a while. But don't throw them away. One day, you will want to have them. Then, you can choose the nicest and . . .'

Molly thought that Abigail would cry at any minute. But Abigail, clutching the frame in her hand, raced down the street as if the hounds of hell were after her.

Molly picked up the wrapping-paper which Abigail had dropped, said a hurried thankyou to Mrs Weathergreen, and raced off in pursuit.

She caught up with Abigail at Silty Bridge – *under* the bridge where it was damp and pebbly, and you could sit and watch the river sliding by. Pleasantly cool on hot days, not so pleasant in October.

Molly slid down the grassy bank, ducked, and settled in beside Abigail. A tractor towing a trailer full of sugar beet rumbled over their heads and the entire bridge bellowed with the noise of it.

'I don't even go to her Sunday School,' Abigail said.

A distant train whistled.

'The 3.42?' Molly asked.

Abigail nodded. They squatted there in silence for a while. Then Abigail said, 'Did you solve the murder mystery while I was away?'

Floor-bricks! Why do I keep forgetting those floor-bricks? 'No,' Molly said. 'But I found an important clue.'

'What is it?'

But Molly wanted to make the most of it. 'I don't want to tell you. I want to *show* you!'

There wasn't time before tea, so they agreed to meet that night. 'Bring your big torch,' Molly said.

'Bring the clues tin,' Abigail said.

'This clue is too big to go in a tin.'

Abigail brightened. 'Ooooh!' she said. 'Sounds exciting! Will you bring Adam?'

'If he wants,' Molly said.

'Where's he gone, by the way?'

'To Ely. On the bus. He needed a new sketch-book. I might go to meet the bus.'

'I'll come too!'

Adam saw Molly and Abigail waiting. He stood up and began to walk to the door, almost falling over as the bus pulled up at the stop.

They've come to meet me, he thought happily.

Molly stepped towards the bus. 'Hello Auntie Phyllis,' she said.

Adam got off the bus and waited with Abigail. While Molly chatted with the conductress, he watched the activities in the street. The vicar carefully walking his bike with an unsteady pile of parish magazines in the basket (you could make a cartoon out of that). A shire horse pulling a train of rusty sheep-hurdles on wheels (greetings card, perhaps). Two soldiers standing on the corner, smoking cigarettes (comic postcard). He lost interest in them almost as soon as he had noticed them. But there was a toddler, covering her ears against the squealing din of the sheep-hurdles. He memorized her for future use – the way she held her head pushed down into her shoulders but with her eyes raised angrily, and her stubborn little legs.

Auntie Phyllis ding-dinged the bell and the bus drew away. As they left the bus-stop, Molly brushed her shoulder against Adam's to show him he was the one she had come to meet really, not her aunt.

'Look!' Adam said.

Hilda Pritt. Standing on the top step of the Crown. Her body turned slightly as she talked to someone inside. Her head cocked with pleasure. One hand resting on her shoulder-bag, the other raised, lightly lifting the back of her hair. Just like they did in the films. A beautiful woman leaving a hotel in New York, turning to wave for a cab.

'Oh, *no*!' Molly said.

'What?'

'If she sees us, we'll have to walk home with her!'

Too late. She'd seen them. She wasn't overjoyed either, but she joined them anyway.

Me with my big sister, Molly thought ironically. Then a little mischief-making devil entered Molly. 'It looked as if you were flirting with someone,' she said.

'Don't be rude, Molly Burns! That's none of your business.'

Molly was polite both by nature and by habit – and that was enough to silence her little devil of malice. Abigail, however, saw that Hilda Pritt quite liked being accused of flirting. 'What *were* you doing there?' she asked.

'Visiting the American pilots, of course!' she said. 'What else?

' – That's where some of them stay.

' – Flights from the wonderful US of A, darlings!

' – Big, big Liberators and beautiful beautiful Boeings.

' – Ciggies, gum, and luvverly luvverly nylon*s*.

' – Not nylon *parachutes*! Don't you kids know *anything*? *Stockings*, darlings! *Nylon* stockings.'

They dawdled, leaving Hilda Pritt to get ahead. Molly pulled Abigail and Adam close to her and, as they huddled, she said, 'Auntie Phyllis told me that Hilda Pritt gets the bus to Little Green every Saturday afternoon. Except when she's away flying.'

It was fun, the three of them sharing a secret in the High Street.

'What's Little Green?'

'It's a small village. Hardly even a village – right beside the air-base.'

Abigail, who had been quiet and low-spirited, suddenly brightened up. 'She's a spy!' she said.

'Perhaps she's got a boyfriend there.'

'Then why does she keep going to the Crown? Unless,' Abigail added darkly, 'she has *lots* of boyfriends.'

'What's so special about nylon stockings anyway?' Molly said later.

None of them knew, so Molly changed the subject. 'I'm taking Abigail to see something after tea,' she said to Adam. 'Want to come?'

'All right,' he said.

'It's a clue,' Abigail said. 'But I don't know what it is. Molly won't tell me.'

When they found it, they didn't know what to do with it. It was not a clue at all, it was another mystery.

Not *it*, actually – *them*. There were three of them. Three new mysteries, all found within a few yards of one another. Three lost things.

Except that they had not been lost – they'd been *stolen*. That's what connected them.

Each was precious in its own way. One was a worthless piece of broken junk believed by its owner to be valuable; one was precious to its owner because it had been made with love; and the third was worth thousands of pounds.

Abigail and Molly were both scared of being out in the black-out. They were familiar with the few hundred yards of street between their homes – one or the other of them often raced alone along that stretch in the dark. But anywhere else frightened them. Adam was not so scared of the dark, but he was uneasy in the open country. But, all three together, they masked their fear by giggling and joking and holding on to each other. That's how they made their way out of the town, along Dead Man's Way, and down the track that led to Paradise Barn.

It was fun. An adventure in the dark – with a small torch dimmed with tissue paper, and carefully pointed to the ground in accordance with blackout regulations. They took with them a second (more powerful) torch (switched off), a candle and some matches. And Cuffey's flapping umbrella.

There was not a single light to be seen anywhere – no car headlights, no window-lights, no streetlights, no stars, no moon. As they drew near to Paradise Barn, its great bulk of blackness loomed over them more solidly than the general darkness which was everywhere else.

The umbrella was not to keep off the rain; it was to hide the light they would have to use. Abigail and Molly both knew that at the top of the church tower the air-raid wardens were watching the darkness for signs of enemy aircraft. If anyone showed a light – however small – it would be seen and there would be trouble.

They stepped cautiously into the Barn. Abigail opened the umbrella and laid it on the floor. The big doors hadn't been closed for years; they were jammed solid and couldn't be moved. Adam shoved and heaved and managed to shift one of them a little. But the other was immovable. So, using the brolly as a shield to hide their light, Molly switched on the brighter torch and searched for the floor-bricks. She found them almost at once – she had been right! They were not perfectly level, and some of them had their rough underside uppermost. They had definitely been disturbed and replaced. One or two of them wobbled a little when she stood on them.

The three of them knelt on the cold floor, studying the bricks. They switched off the torch and lit the candle instead. The darkness closed in around them and they huddled in the candlelight while Molly explained about the bricks.

They tried to lift them out but they fitted too tightly together. It was not possible to get a grip on them with their fingers. They needed something sharp, a blade of some kind to slip between the bricks.

So Abigail ventured out of the candle-light to search among the jumble of farm stuff that was always in the barn. She felt as if she was travelling to the outer edges of the universe. 'Keep talking to me,' she whispered.

In the shadowy candle-twilight Abigail searched. And almost immediately they heard her gasp. Then she hurried back to the others. 'Look what I've found!' she said.

A shovel with a broken handle – and Molly and Abigail recognised it immediately. Charlie Leggett's missing shovel, the one with the Viking history.

'So that's where it got to!'

They managed to push the blade of the shovel between two of the bricks and prise them up. After that, it was easy. The bricks were not cemented in place, just resting on dry powdery earth. Within a couple of minutes they had cleared about a square yard of floor.

They used the shovel to dig out the earth. This proved harder than they had expected because the blade hit a solid object only an inch or two down. It felt and sounded like something made of wood. After that, it was easier to scoop out the dry earth with their hands.

'Treasure!' Abigail whispered.

It was a large flat object. When they had cleared away more of the earth they could see that it had four metal fitments, one at each corner. Its wooden surface was scuffed and soiled, but Molly recognised it at once.

'Mrs Weathergreen's flower-press!'

'That's why someone stole Charlie Leggett's shovel – because they needed to dig this hole!' Abigail whispered, working it out.

'But why would anyone want to . . . ?'

They could make no sense of this. Their bright familiar world was opening into dark mysteries. They lifted the flower-press out of the hole, undid the brass fasteners and took off the top. Pressed inside there were layers of white blotting paper and a few wisps of flattened grass.

'There's something else.'

There was another layer, a little thicker than the blotting paper sheets. The girls pulled it out to see.

'It's a painting!'

'Perhaps it belongs to Mrs Weathergreen?'

But Adam recognised it. 'It's the one in the newspaper.' His throat was so constricted that he almost choked as he said the words. 'The one that was stolen in Paris.'

Abigail had never seen the item of news about the stolen painting. But Molly had, and she peered closely. 'Yes, it is!' she whispered. In the bottom right-hand corner, she read *Camille Pissarro 1882*.

They tried to explain it all to Abigail. As they did so, a new knowledge began to possess them. They had been pretending all along, playing a game, being detectives. But there was another game, more dangerous, with different rules. It was a grown-up game – and now they were caught in it.

The sensible thing was to take the painting and the flower-press home and hand the matter over to adults. Or even to the police station. It would have been perfectly easy – *See what we found! We noticed that the floor had been disturbed. So we dug there and this is what we found!* They would be praised and admired all round. They might even be in the newspapers.

Afterwards, they were never quite sure why they decided not to do that. Something drew them deeper in. Something in the mystery itself. Or something in themselves, wanting to find out about wickedness.

They decided that they must hide two of the stolen objects somewhere safe. It seemed the essential and obvious thing to do. They half-believed that this was because Adam wanted to have a proper look at the painting in daylight. But, in fact, Adam never said that.

None of them could remember how they came to agree to their plan. It was settled in seconds. Charlie Leggett's shovel could be left in the barn. They would tell him they had seen it there and he would be overjoyed. But the flower-press and the painting had to be hidden safely away for the time being.

But where?

'One of the caravans.' Just making the suggestion made Molly feel like a criminal.

The caravans in Bunty Fen belonged to Mr and Mrs Spinks and were used by people on fishing holidays. They were small rounded two-wheeled trailers. Molly and Abigail used to help to get them clean on Saturday afternoons when one lot of fishermen had left and the next lot had not yet arrived. They earned two shillings each. Because of the War, no-one had come this year –

but the twelve empty caravans still stood there, close to the river. Molly and Abigail both knew where the keys were kept.

Hastily, they swept the dirt back into the hole and replaced the bricks. It was an untidy job but they were in too much of a hurry to mind. They blew out the candle and closed the umbrella. The darkness seemed even more total than before. Nevertheless, with the painting safely back inside the flower-press, they set off.

No giggles this time, no laughter. They whispered anxiously to each other and held each other's arms, or bits of clothing. Twice the flower-press got dropped. It was awkward to carry.

Bunty Fen was about half a mile from the barn, along a field-path. They climbed a stile, climbed two more at the railway, and finally stepped warily across a narrow plank footbridge over a small deep stream.

The caravans stood in deep wet grass like twelve mis-shapen elephants grazing silently. Molly and Abigail found the keys. That was easy; they hung on their usual nail inside the wooden shed which Mr and Mrs Spinks used as an office.

They chose number seven because it was furthest away from the gate, close to the river-bank. They unlocked the door, stumbled in, and risked switching on the torch. The air was damp and stale, and it felt even colder than outside. When they moved to the far end their weight tipped the caravan down and it settled with a soft thump. That startled them rather. The flower-press was stuffed under a mattress and in no time they were outside again and locking the door.

'Give me the keys,' Abigail said. She detached the key to number seven and slipped it into her pocket. 'We'll keep that,' she said.

'But what if the Spinks come . . . ?'

'They won't. They haven't been near the place since the War broke out.'

The way back took them close to Paradise Barn again. But as they approached it Molly made them stop.

They listened intently. From somewhere across the Fens came the faint (almost inaudible) sound of an air-raid warning. From forty miles away, maybe. They waited for others to join in, for the drone of approaching enemy bombers.

But there were no more air-raid warnings, and no planes. Other people were getting the bombs that night. Peterborough perhaps. But in the silence Molly heard something else. She hushed the others and pulled them down. They crouched as low as they could.

They listened.

Almost certainly, they heard sounds of something moving in the barn. Or someone. It might have been a hedgehog. Or an art thief. Or a murderer.

'A *hedgehog*?' Adam said in disbelief.

'Ssssh!' Abigail whispered. 'Yes! Hedgehogs can be very noisy.'

Then there was silence again, and they began to think

they had imagined it. After a long wait, they carried on, close by the barn and into the town.

With relief, they burst into Mrs Barnes' bright kitchen. They were excited now, keyed up, finding it hard to keep secrets. But there was no time for anything else that evening. They were late, Mrs Barnes said, and Abigail must go straight home. She was not keen on letting Molly or Adam out into the dark any more that day, so she offered to go with Abigail herself.

'I'll go with her if you like.' It was Hilda Pritt. 'I've only just come in. I've still got my coat on.'

Mrs Barnes did not conceal her surprise. 'Well, if . . .'

'Come on, Abigail, I don't want to hang around for ever.'

Molly whispered into Abigail's ear, 'Don't let her get you talking!'

Abigail whispered back: 'I intend to get *her* talking!'

'What about?'

'Nylon stockings.'

Ten minutes later, Hilda Pritt arrived back and took off her overcoat.

Tuesday 22ⁿᵈ October ~ half-term holiday

The next morning, Adam received his weekly letter. He always called them 'letters from home', though in fact he hadn't got a home any more. His dad's letters were brief: all they said was that he was all right and he hoped that Adam was too. His mum's were more interesting, telling Adam about her training – shorthand, typing and map-reading, but never aeroplanes. The best came from his grandmother, who still lived in North London. She gave detailed accounts of the bombing and Adam would spread out an old street map of London and find the places she mentioned. 'Poor old Katherine's Dock copped it again Thursday night,' she wrote. Or it might be Brunswick Gardens, a church near Leicester Square, Upper Berkeley Street, the Freemasons' pub in Portobello Road.

Adam found them all, and grimly crayoned in small star-shaped explosions on the map.

After breakfast, they went back to the caravan and spread out the painting on the table. Then they elbowed each other onto the tiny caravan seat so that they could all three look at it.

What struck Adam was the colour. Its brightness burned itself into his mind, left him almost breathless. It blazed like a beacon. In his heart he honoured it, but – for a boy who drew black-and-white pictures in pencil – it was a beacon at the summit of a very lofty mountain. He studied it thoughtfully, longingly.

Abigail saw the people in it. There were only three: a young peasant woman was walking with a heavy basket, and a younger child – a girl of about five or six – was following her. The girl was looking back at the third figure, approaching them from a distant village. He was a soldier, with a musket over his shoulder and a large shapeless bundle. Was he a threat? Or was it a home-coming? What was about to happen? Abigail turned round, knelt up on the seat, pressed her nose against the window and stared out at the relentless autumn rain.

As for Molly, she thought the picture was quite nice. Especially the blue sky with white clouds. And the beautiful slender trees. But she had seen plenty of others that she thought were just as good – on birthday cards, in books, sometimes on people's walls. She couldn't see why this one was so good that it had been hung in a famous gallery in Paris. What was special about it? What made it so important that someone had stolen it? Was there some secret clue so that clever people always knew when a painting was a great work of art?

She lost interest. What was more important to Molly

was the flower-press. 'We've got to give the flower-press back to Mrs Weathergreen,' she said. 'As soon as we can.'

There was no answer, so she went outside into the rain and round to the window where Abigail still had her nose pressed white and flat on the glass, like the underside of a snail. Molly put out her tongue at Abigail. Abigail drew back and put out her tongue at Molly. Then Abigail put her tongue *on* the glass. *Yukk!* thought Molly. Then she did it too, tasting rain.

Back in the caravan, she said again, 'We've got to get the flower-press back to Mrs Weathergreen. *We* have it – and *she's* unhappy without it.'

Abigail was still gloomy. 'But if we just take it to her, she'll think we stole it.'

There was some truth in this and Molly and Abigail argued about it for several minutes.

Suddenly Adam said, 'Come on!'

Abigail and Molly exchanged ironic glances, which meant: *he's being decisive.*

But they didn't mind decisiveness when it served their purpose. Adam put the painting between some of Mrs Weathergreen's blotting-paper and placed it back in its hiding-place under the seat. There was an old oil-cloth spread over the small caravan table; he took this and wrapped the flower-press in it like a parcel.

Back they went, traipsing across the sodden field, along the muddy footpath, into the outskirts of Great Deeping, along the High Street, around the corner and so to Mrs Weathergreen's cottage. Shoes, socks and the hems of skirts got soaked. It was not a comfortable walk because the flower-press was too big to be tucked under one arm. None of them had arms long enough. So it had to be carried in other ways, all of them awkward.

But they arrived. And Adam made the two girls hide around the corner with the flower-press, out of sight from Mrs Weathergreen's front door. They ducked behind a water-butt and under a dripping elder tree. It was a mucky business.

Adam rang the bell.

Mrs Weathergreen opened the door and looked at him for a moment. 'You're Molly Barnes' evacuee, aren't you?'

'Yes. I'm Adam Swales.'

'What can I do for you, Adam?' Mrs Weathergreen said with interest.

'We have something for you, but first you must make a promise.'

We? Mrs Weathergreen looked quickly around her front garden. Who was this *we*? She waited for Adam to continue.

'Before we give it to you, you have to promise to believe anything we tell you.'

'Don't be ridiculous, young man. How could anyone with any sense make such a promise? Why, you might tell me you had been to the moon and back!'

Adam was taken by surprise. She was supposed to be just a kindly old lady – she had no right to turn shrewish. 'It's important,' he said. 'You *must* promise to believe what we tell you.' There was a hint of desperation in his voice.

'I shall make no such promise at all,' Mrs Weathergreen said. Then she raised her voice as if she was addressing Sunday School. 'But I can tell you this: I will probably believe anything Molly Barnes tells me. Not because of any silly promises but because I trust her.'

Adam knew when he was defeated. He went to the corner and beckoned to Molly and Abigail to come out. And, in spite of the oil-cloth wrapping, Mrs Weathergreen knew at once what they were carrying. The three children were welcomed in, taken into Mrs Weathergreen's warm living-room, made to rub their wet hair on a towel, given biscuits and squash, and generally made a fuss of.

The old lady was overjoyed to have her flower-press back.

'We found it,' Molly said, 'but you must believe us – we didn't steal it.'

'I didn't think you did,' Mrs Weathergreen said. 'But where did you find it?'

'There's an old barn on our side of the town. We play in it sometimes. And we found it there.'

'Mr Morton's barn? I know it well. I used to play there myself when I was little. But how did my flower-press get there?'

They speculated and guessed and gossiped for almost an hour. 'Why is it called Paradise Barn?' Abigail said.

'When I was a girl,' Mrs Weathergreen said, 'I thought it *was* Paradise. I had such happy times there! But later, when I was married, I found out that its old name was Purdy's Barn.'

Three pairs of shoes and three pairs of socks were arranged neatly on the hearth, steaming as they dried. The steam joined the smoke from the fire and slid tidily up into the chimney.

'My husband was interested in the history of the town. He found out that the barn used to belong to a farmer called Jonathan Purdy. Then the Purdys all died out or went away. They were forgotten and the name gradually changed from Purdy's to Paradise.'

After a pause, Mrs Weathergreen said thoughtfully, 'My name is carved on one of the walls.'

'You carved your name?' Molly was very interested.

'Well, no, Molly. I didn't say *I* carved it.'

I'll look for it, Molly thought. When all this business is over. 'What was your name?' she said.

'I was Laura Wainwright then.' For some reason Mrs Weathergreen blushed as she said it. All the time, she was contentedly rubbing wax polish into her beloved flower-press.

The children said nothing about the painting.

The rain had stopped and there were patches of pale blue sky when they set off home. As they passed the Crown Hotel they had another encounter with Hilda

Pritt. She was talking to a man on the steps of the hotel. An air-force jeep stood at the curbside.

'Again!' muttered the outraged Abigail. 'How many men-friends does she need?'

Hilda saw them and waved gaily. 'I have another flight to make,' she said as they came near. 'I have to go! Somewhere in bloomin' Scotland! I'm not supposed to say really. But you aren't spies, are you!' Hilda laughed in her silly Prittish way.

'*You* might be, though!' Abigail muttered.

A voice came from inside the jeep. A man's voice. American. 'Come on, honey! If you want a ride to the air-base, we have to go – right now!'

'Bye kids!' Hilda cried gaily. 'I'll be back on Friday.'

'In time to make her Saturday trip to Little Green,' Abigail said to the others as they watched the jeep roar out of town.

'Do you *really* think so?' Molly said. She meant the question seriously. It was no longer so easy to know what was a game and what was real.

Adam said nothing. Again, his mind's eye saw Hilda Pritt, leather-helmeted, at an altitude of several thousand feet, with rain and cloud streaming past her as she navigated a stuttering Hurricane towards a distant airfield somewhere in the north. Alone, concentrating – certainly not giggling.

Molly stopped them. 'I've just thought!'

'What?'

'We can't just let Charlie Leggett go and get his shovel.'

'Why not?' Adam said, only half-interested.

'It's probably got the murderer's finger-prints on it. The police will want . . . '

She never finished her sentence. Realisation came over them. 'It's got *our* finger-prints all over it!' Molly said.

'Especially mine!' Abigail said.

'But it won't matter,' Adam said. 'It's obvious that our prints are likely to be on it – we found it!'

But Abigail's thoughts were moving in a different direction. 'Wait a sec! If the murderer used the shovel to bury the painting, why hasn't he come back to get it?'

Molly had a different idea. 'Perhaps it was the murdered man who buried it. Before he got killed.'

They gave up. It was too muddled.

'We need a council of war,' Abigail said. 'To look at all the clues and sort things out!'

Just like her mum, Molly thought. *She* likes things sorted out too.

Wednesday 23rd October ~ back to school

Their council of war was a bad-tempered business. This was partly because of Molly, who wouldn't stop grumbling. 'We'll all get sent to prison for keeping a stolen painting,' she insisted. 'Why can't we just hand it in?'

But Abigail seemed to enjoy the risk. 'No, we won't,' she said. 'Stop fussing!'

'I'm *not* fussing!' Molly wailed. And so it went on.

Adam just said they'd find a way and she needn't worry about it.

Molly felt excluded. There was a small cross resentment inside her. This never happened when it was just the two of us, Abigail and me, she thought.

She felt like a thief. All three of them were thieves. And she couldn't understand the other two. Why couldn't they see it?

The council of war took place after school, in the shed at the bottom of Abigail's garden. Abigail was being bossy. 'We need to write down all the clues,' she said. 'Study the evidence.'

Molly agreed gloomily and Abigail went on. 'We've got two crimes here and we haven't solved either of them,' she said crossly.

'*Two* crimes?' Molly said.

'The murder and the stolen painting.'

'But they're the same crime.'

Abigail pushed her chin back and screwed up her face. In Abigail's language of facial expressions this meant *cross*, *baffled* and *daft*: Abigail was cross and baffled; Molly's suggestion was daft.

Molly explained. 'They're not separate crimes, they're different bits of the same crime. It's obvious – because of the French!'

Abigail paid attention properly. So did Adam.

'The murdered man was a French art-dealer. The painting was stolen in France.'

'And one of the bits of evidence,' Adam said, 'was a bill from a French café. Molly's right.'

Abigail liked to regard herself as the logical one, the clear-thinking one. But she could see that Molly was right. 'Well,' she said grudgingly, 'we need to write out a list of everything we know. Can I have a sheet of paper from your sketch-book, Adam?'

She reached out to tear a page from Adam's book.

'Oi! Leave my sketch-book alone, you!' Adam grabbed her wrist.

'I only want one page from it! To write on.'

Adam was outraged. 'Well, you can't have it! It's special paper for drawing on.'

'Oh, well, if . . . '

Molly hurriedly found a scrap of paper and they began to make a list.

1 THE PAINTING WAS STOLEN FROM PARIS IN JUNE
2 THE DEAD MAN WAS A FRENCH ART-DEALER (MR DUFOUR)
3 THE BILL CAME FROM A CAFÉ IN PARIS IN FEBRUARY
4 THERE WERE SMALL ROUND HOLES IN THE MUD
5 THE FLOWER-PRESS WAS STOLEN ON THE SAME DAY AS THE MURDER
6 THAT WAS THE DAY THE GERMANS WERE SUPPOSED TO INVADE (ONLY THEY DIDN'T)

They added what they still called the bit of knicker-elastic, though it had been found so far along the path that it might be nothing to do with the murder.

7 THE PIECE OF BLACK ELASTIC (PERHAPS)

Then they began to speculate. What, Adam wanted to know, had the thief intended to do with the stolen painting? He would have to get it out of the country – but how could that be done in wartime?

'I suppose he could send it by post,' Abigail suggested.

'*Can* you send things overseas in wartime?'

'My mum gets letters from her cousin in New York,' Adam said. 'And she writes back. The War hasn't stopped that.'

But you couldn't send a stolen painting by post, they thought. All parcels would be examined because of the War.

Another puzzle: if the thief had been killed for the painting, why didn't the murderer just take it away with him afterwards? Why trouble to bury it and then leave it?

Or, if the painting had been buried not by the murderer but by the victim, why didn't the killer find out first where it was hidden and kill him afterwards?

'And what about the long grass?'

The other two turned to Molly. '*What* long grass?'

'Mrs Weathergreen's flower-press was stolen on the same day as the murder. But someone told Mrs Weathergreen that they'd seen the press later in the long grass behind the church hall. But when they went to look next day it had gone.'

Neither Adam nor Abigail thought this mattered much.

Molly tried to explain why it mattered to her. But she failed. She couldn't make them understand. The only way she could make a sensible account of these details was if she could *see* the story happening in her head. The flower-press in the long grass had to be fitted into this story.

Then they began to list suspects.

NUMBER 1 ~ HILDA PRITT.

She was an obvious choice. They already suspected her of spying on the air-base near Little Green, and she admitted she had flown planes to and from France. She could have brought the painting to England as her part of the crime. Besides, they didn't like her.

NUMBER 2 ~ CUFFEY.

It was Adam who thought Cuffey should be included in the list. But there was no evidence against him. Molly remembered that Cuffey had once been in love with a

French girlfriend but she said nothing. She kept her private conversations with Cuffey to herself; she'd not even told Abigail about them. Cuffey is *my* friend, not theirs, Molly thought. Besides, it was too long ago to count.

NUMBER 3 ~ GERMAN PRISONERS–OF–WAR.

One of them might have been a killer. After all, they *were* Nazis. But it was hard to see how one of them could have been an art-thief. 'Most of them came from a German U-boat that had been sunk by the Royal Navy,' Molly said. 'How could they have kept the painting dry?'

'There are a few captured pilots there as well,' Adam said. He had been talking to his aircraft-buddies at school.

NUMBER 4 ~ MRS WEATHERGREEN.

It was Mrs Weathergreen's flower-press. She could have killed the Frenchman, stolen the painting, and used her flower-press to hide it in until the enquiry had died down.

But they were half-hearted about Mrs Weathergreen. They knew she wasn't a murderer.

'Anyway,' Molly went on, 'there has to be a motive for a crime as well.'

'Greed,' Abigail said. 'The thief was going to sell it for *thousands* of pounds.'

'Dollars, probably,' Adam said. 'In America.'

'But how was he going to get it there?'

Adam had been looking vaguely out of the shed

window. It was Molly who noticed that his look suddenly sharpened. She nudged Abigail and they both shouldered themselves close to Adam so that they could all three look out of the small pane of cobwebby glass.

Across the fields, about half a mile away, they could see Paradise Barn. Someone was walking rapidly towards it. He was a big man, wearing boots and combat trousers. He stopped when he reached the barn, looked it up and down, and then went inside.

Their bad temper vanished. Abigail raced off and came back almost at once with a pair of binoculars. 'My dad's,' she said. 'He was a bird-watcher.'

Molly noticed the *was*. She couldn't tell if Abigail had noticed it herself. Abigail got the binoculars into focus and they passed them from person to person, whispering to each other as if they believed the stranger might hear them.

He was in the barn for almost an hour. To the children, it seemed an unbelievably long time. When he finally came out, they passed the binoculars frantically from one to the other. When it was Molly's turn, she was almost scared by the way the distant figure leapt into closeness. He seemed at one moment to be looking straight at her from only a few feet away.

She gave the glasses to Adam. 'I know who he is,' she said. 'I've seen him coming out of the Crown Hotel.'

'Another suspect,' Abigail said.

'I suppose so, but . . . ' Molly was unsure.

Abigail protested. 'He's spent nearly an hour in the

barn! *Why?* Unless he's interested in old farm-yard junk, why would he do that?'

'That doesn't mean he's a murderer,' Molly said.

'No, but it does mean he's interested in the painting,' Adam pointed out.

It seemed impossible to argue with that.

He does *look* like a murderer, Molly thought. Big, immensely strong. And he looked menacing and violent, Molly's idea of a bully. The man had a map in his hands, loosely folded. He stood outside the barn and studied it, smacking it down angrily when it flapped in the wind. He turned and looked back towards the town. Then he looked across towards the river – to Bunty Fen, where the caravans were. They could see he was very thoughtful.

'If he goes to the caravans, he'll find it,' Abigail muttered.

But he didn't. He looked at his wristwatch, stuffed the map into a pocket low in his trouser-leg, and hurried back towards the town, almost at a run.

For a few breathless minutes they couldn't stop talking – a muddle of excited words and dramatic suggestions. But out of it came the realisation that the painting had to be moved. The stranger had left the caravans for another time – but it was clear that he intended to come back.

'But where can we hide it?' Molly wailed.

'In the barn,' Adam said.

At first, the girls thought this was ridiculous.

'He's already searched there. He won't look there again.'

Back at Molly's house, they went to a cupboard in one of the upstairs rooms where Mrs Barnes kept a collection of old toys and oddments for young children staying at the guesthouse. Molly remembered that there were some old cardboard tubes among the jumble of objects. They found one: it had been bashed about – used as a trumpet, a weapon, the tower of an army fort, and a tunnel for toy trains. Someone had written on it in red crayon *Death to the Queen*. But the cardboard was tough and thick, almost as strong as wood, and it was about the right size for the stolen painting.

So, rolled up and safely stowed in the tube, Pissarro's oil painting was taken back to Paradise Barn that night, after dark, and hidden not in the floor this time, but deep inside an ancient crumbling threshing-machine.

A few more floor-bricks had been torn up. And not put back.

Thursday 24ᵗʰ October ~ after school

Abigail wanted to re-establish her position as the Person in Charge of Logic and Clear Thinking.

'See that tin of paints,' she said, pointing.

It was in the window of Mr Woodruff's toyshop, a large flat wooden box, with paintbrushes and oil paints in tubes, and small blocks of colour. Very expensive.

'Suppose we wanted to steal it.'

'But we don't,' Molly said quickly.

'I *know*! But just suppose we did want to. How could we do it?'

'Well, there's no-one in the shop at the moment,' Adam said, 'and the shop-bell wouldn't ring because the door's open.'

'So how would you do it?' Abigail demanded.

'I'd walk inside, pick it up when he wasn't looking, and walk out again.'

'You might be very good at drawing pictures, Adam Swales, but you'd be no good at stealing things.'

Adam pulled a face.

'What would you do next?' Abigail said. 'Put it in your pocket?'

'It's too big.'

'So what *would* you do with it?'

They stood there for a moment in silence – as Molly and Adam came to realise that there were always people in the High Street. A thief couldn't walk through the street with a large wooden paint-box under his arm without people noticing. If a policeman questioned them, they would remember.

Abigail put on a gruff policeman's voice. 'Miss Robinson, on the afternoon of 24th October at about 4.00 p.m. did you see anyone carrying a large flat object that might have been the missing paint-box?'

She answered herself in a Miss Robinson voice, high and wavering. 'Well, now I come to think about it, officer, there was a boy carrying something like that. My eyes are not very good at my age, but you could hardly miss him, with an object as big as that. One of those blooming evacuees. Up to no good, I'll be bound.'

'Who's Miss Robinson?' Molly asked with interest.

'I made her up.'

Adam turned back to the shop-window, thinking.

'So how could you do it?' Abigail said.

'I know!' Adam said. 'I'd take it out of the shop now, while no-one is in there. Then slip it behind some of that rubbish there.'

Beside the shop there was a passage where Mr Woodruff kept his rubbish-bins and some piles of cardboard.

'Then I'd wait till it was dark and come back and collect it.'

'He might find it there before you came back for it.'

'I'd have to risk that.'

Molly realised what Abigail had been getting at. 'That's why the flower-press was in the long grass.'

Abigail jumped up and down on the pavement. '*Yes!*' she cried. 'At *last!*'

Molly continued slowly, putting the story together. 'The art thief saw the press in the lavatory behind the church hall. He realised it would be ideal for what he wanted. So he took it out. But he couldn't carry it through the town in broad daylight because there were people about and they would see him. So he hid it in the long grass and came back for it when there was no-one about.'

Molly and Adam were impressed but Abigail had already lost her cheerfulness. 'It doesn't help us much, does it?' she admitted.

Molly tried to cheer her. 'You *are* clever! And it must help if we understand how everything was done.'

'I wonder if it could be done . . .' Adam said.

The two girls continued on their way along the street. Molly was beginning to realise that Abigail's thinking really did help. 'It means,' she said excitedly, 'that the thief was walking around the town when it was still daylight. To pass the time, he went into the hall to see Mrs Weathergreen's display of wild flowers and went to the lav at the back.'

Abigail brightened up. 'He saw the flower-press

there and thought *I could use that to put the painting in when I hide it.'*

Now Molly could almost see how it happened. 'So he took the press into the long grass, quickly, when no-one was about.'

'And came back for it later.'

'I doubt if he waited until it was completely dark, though. It was mid-summer and it didn't get dark for ages.'

'It rained later, remember. So nobody would have been about.'

'How do you know it rained?' Molly asked.

'I remember,' Abigail answered. 'It was the night they rang the church bells. Because of the invasion. Everyone was indoors listening to the wireless.'

'I wonder if it *was* a Frenchman,' Molly said dreamily.

'The whole thing only happened because he went into the lav at the back of the hall,' Abigail said. She thought it strange that such big things depended on such small ones.

'He needed a *oui oui*,' Molly said. It was the kind of joke they might have made when they were six. So they laughed at it as if they were still six – helplessly, stupidly, doubled up until it hurt, clutching each other.

But they recovered themselves. 'Come on, Adam!' Molly shouted back.

It was dark when Abigail left Molly's house to go home. Molly went to the side gate with her. She would watch while Abigail raced through the darkness. They didn't know where Adam had got to.

There was a bright moon that night. A bomber's moon, people called it.

They heard footsteps, someone running. Adam was coming from the other direction. As he came up to them, they could see that he was carrying something.

'You were right,' he said breathlessly. 'It *can* be done!'

Saturday 26ᵗʰ October

They became increasingly suspicious of Hilda Pritt.
Now that they knew she took the bus most Saturdays to
Little Green, they were convinced she was up to no
good. She was a spy, perhaps. Or an art thief. Possibly a
murderer. Little Green was close to one of the biggest
air-bases in East Anglia. Its perimeter fence ran along
the bottom of some of the village back gardens.

'Why don't we follow her?'

'On the bus?'

'She'd see us! Only about three people go to Little
Green.'

'Only about ten people live there!'

It was Abigail who came up with a realistic plan. 'We
could cycle there before the bus goes and lie in wait till
she gets there. It's only about five miles. Then we'll
watch her in the village and find out what she does.'

That was the plan – and it worked. They had to
borrow Mrs Barnes' bike for Adam to ride, and
everything went well – except that Adam found it hard
to cycle across open country roads against a relentless
headwind.

But they arrived before the bus and hid themselves

and their bikes behind the wall of the churchyard. Hilda Pritt – with her head high and dressed to the nines in her civvy clothes – left the bus, crossed the village green and went to the front door of a small cottage.

'Doesn't seem a very likely place for spies to meet,' Molly said doubtfully.

'The less likely it seems, the better it is,' Adam said.

There was no arguing with that.

Abigail was being decisive that day. She didn't hesitate. She led them into the village shop, used her coupons to buy three kit-kats, and engaged the shop-keeper in conversation.

'Can you tell us where Miss Barley lives, please?'

Barley? What was she on about?

'Barley?' said the shop-keeper. 'Een't no-one called Barley round here.'

'Oh. We thought she lived in that little cottage across the green,' Abigail said.

'No. Nobody called Barley lives there! That's Edie Pritt's house.'

Edie Pritt. They stared, taking it in.

'Poor old thing she is now. Howsomever, her grand-daughter visits her regular, and she really looks forward to that. Real good to her grandma she is, that gal!'

That evening, round at Abigail's house, Adam drew a cartoon. There was an aeroplane flying high, a two-seater. In the front was Hilda Pritt, in leather helmet and goggles; behind her sat a huge old lady, with a wicked grin on her face, waving a walking-stick in the air. There was a caption underneath: *CAN'T YOU MAKE THIS THING GO FASTER, HILDA!*

'Abigail, what made you think of Miss *Barley*?'

'There were barley-sugars in a jar.'

Later Abigail said, 'Of course, the fact that Hilda Pritt's granny lives in Little Green doesn't mean that Hilda is *not* a spy.'

But the others weren't convinced.

Once a week, Mrs Barnes allowed her family (and guests if they wanted it) a fish-and-chip supper. It was a tradition started by Molly's dad, years ago, before the War. This week, Cuffey offered to go for the fish-and-chips if Molly would keep him company. The fish-shop was at the other end of the town.

As they walked home through the dark streets, the newspaper bundle that Cuffey carried under his arm trailed its familiar promising smell.

Molly, walking happily beside him, said, 'Tell me about your first girlfriend – the French one.'

'Hélène?'

'Yes, Hélène.'

'What do you want to know?'

'Well, what was she like?'

'Thoughtful,' Cuffey said. 'Remote. As if she had another world in her head – a private world.'

Molly absorbed this. 'You told me she was ten. But how old were you?'

'About the same. We were in the same class at school.'

'You said you were an apprentice lover. Did you

really love her?' (How dare she ask such things? she wondered.)

Cuffey thought for a moment. 'Yes, desperately,' he said. 'Children can love as desperately as grown-ups, I think. There is no difference.'

'Did you tell her?'

'No. That *is* a difference. Children don't tell each other.'

Nobody else talked to Molly about being in love. When she and Cuffey discussed big grown-up themes, she felt as if her life were expanding, opening out to meet the bigger world.

'Who were the other three?' she asked. (Would he tell?)

Although it was dark, Molly sensed that he was smiling a little. 'Marie was the first. She was a dancer, a lovely lovely dancer! Every man in Paris was in love with her! But she was hard of heart. She hurt me badly and it took me three years to recover. Ridiculous, really. Then came the second, Charlotte. She was British – and we were married for a few years. But . . .'

(What happened? Oh, *please* tell me!)

Cuffey would say no more about Charlotte.

(All right, then. I'll try something else.) 'Who was the last one?' she asked him.

'The last one was Hélène.'

'Another Hélène?'

'No. The same Hélène. I went back and fell in love with her all over again.'

(Or perhaps he hadn't ever stopped.) 'Perhaps you hadn't ever stopped?' Molly said.

Cuffey slowed in his walking and looked down at her. 'Yes,' he said thoughtfully. 'I think you may be right.'

'What happened?'

'I had left it too late.'

(I *knew* he had some great sadness.)

Molly longed to know more, but Cuffey had come to a fullstop on that subject. Nothing she said would induce him to tell her more about Hélène. Molly didn't know what she wanted to know – but she did know there were grown-up secrets to be uncovered.

(I'll try a different tack.)

'When you were a boy,' she said, 'were you bad?'

'No, not very,' he said. 'I stole apricots from the village priest's conservatory – that sort of thing. But nothing very bad.'

'Were you punished a lot?'

'Yes, I was. But the punishments did no good. They never made me feel ashamed or guilty.'

'What do you mean?'

'They just made me more cunning about not getting caught. Guilt came later.'

Molly still didn't understand.

'I crossed over from childhood. Then came guilt. And secrets.'

'What did you do?' Molly asked. (Was it something to do with Hélène?)

'We are all guilty, we adults. We can't be trusted, Molly. And, God help us, we are your teachers!'

(He's gone off on some idea of his own!) 'But what did you do?'

'I can't tell you.'

'Did you have lots of shameful secrets?' (I wish I could tell him about the painting. *My* secret.)

'Not lots. You only need one to destroy your peace of mind. That's when you stop being a child.'

Cuffey patted her lightly on the top of the head.

(Have I stopped being a child? I wish he wouldn't do that.)

'It's hard to explain. You are so innocent – but one day you will understand.'

(I'm not as innocent as he thinks.) 'I'm quite a bad person,' she said quietly.

He slowed a little and turned towards her in the dark empty street. 'My little Molly,' he said gently, 'surely *you* don't have guilty secrets?'

(He's laughing at me.)

She changed the subject. 'Have you got any children?' she asked.

Cuffey didn't answer but Molly persisted. 'Cuffey?' she said.

Then Cuffey said heavily, 'I used to have.'

(*Used to have*? What did *that* mean?)

'I had a daughter, once.'

Molly didn't know what to say. Suppose he told her she had died? Or been captured by the enemy? Were you supposed to hug someone? What did grown-ups *do* – and what did they *say* – when they were told about something really sad? She was afraid she'd get it wrong and make it worse for him.

So she asked no more questions about his lost daughter. But she stored the information in her mind, alongside the other Cuffey mysteries.

'Molly, why all these questions? What are you trying to find out?'

Molly thought for a moment. 'I don't know,' she said truthfully.

Later, when she was in bed, she realised with some interest that her share in that conversation had been in two separate parts. What she thought had not been the same as what she had said. Was she turning into a different person? A hypocrite? Or had she always been like that and had only just noticed?

She didn't mind about herself. But then it occurred to her that Cuffey might be capable of the same thing. Or perhaps everybody did it.

That was a truly shocking thought but, as it was forming itself, she fell asleep.

That day there was a truly terrible row at the Ely Guesthouse.

Molly went into Hilda Pritt's room and found a gun there. Then Hilda went in and found Molly.

Later, in the gathering darkness of the afternoon, Abigail was standing on the fence at the bottom of her garden, talking to the man in the guard's van at the back of a freight train. It had 52 wagons (Abigail had counted them) and had stopped across the level-crossing. The guard was a friend of Abigail's.

She heard the clang of the signal being lowered to *GO*. Then, after a whistle from the engine, there was a great clattering and banging of metal as the train began to ease away. The guard waved goodbye and, as Abigail jumped backwards off the fence, she saw Adam running down the garden towards her.

This was unusual. Abigail had been expecting Molly.

'Molly's been sent to bed with nothing to eat until breakfast. She found a gun in Hilda Pritt's room!'

Among her mother's cabbages and leeks, Abigail stood open-mouthed, waiting to hear all about it.

'A *gun*?'

After school, Molly had gone past Hilda Pritt's bedroom and glanced in. She saw her own Sooty curled up comfortably with Adam's three-legged cat on Hilda's bed. This was not allowed and Molly went in to remove them. That was not allowed either, but Molly thought that under the circumstances she was justified.

On the floor by the bed stood Hilda's big leather shoulder-bag, open, and in it – on top of all the other contents – was a small revolver. Molly froze. A gun in their house! She couldn't believe it. Instead of the cats, it was the gun she picked up. She held it gingerly in the palm of her hand.

She had always believed there were special guns for women, delicate, made of polished silver, with mother-of-pearl handles. But this one had an ugly blunt shape, and it was made of a hard blueish metal. It had a brown horn-like grip with the word *Webley* on it, and criss-crossed grooves in it. The barrel was about three inches long.

That was how Hilda Pritt found Molly, standing in her room with the gun in her hand.

Then the row started. There were tears, protestations of innocence, accusations of injustice. Adam had stood by, a fascinated observer. And, when Molly had been sent away to get into her pyjamas and stay in her bedroom, he set off to tell Abigail about it.

Through all this, the cats slept contentedly on Hilda Pritt's bed. 'And *you* can get out of my room too!' Hilda said. 'Go on, both of you! *Shoo!*'

Later, when Adam was having a bedtime biscuit in the kitchen, Molly came downstairs in her pyjamas. Her face was white and tear-stained. Even her bare feet, Adam thought, somehow managed to look tragic. She rushed to her mum and held her passionately.

Mrs Barnes held Molly's face in front of her. She spoke firmly still, but with a hint of relenting. 'It's all right, Molly. Go back to bed now.'

'But . . . ' Molly wanted more than that.

'We'll say no more about it.'

'Can I have a biscuit, please?'

'Yes.'

Molly took one and went gloomily back to bed. She knew she was only half-forgiven. But, then, she had been very rude to Miss Pritt.

They were walking home from school, in the High Street. Adam was bad-tempered and moody, as he had been the day before. Abigail and Molly were discussing whether Hilda Pritt should be moved to the top of their list of suspects.

'Why?' Adam asked, only half interested.

'The murdered man was shot,' Abigail said.

'And now we know that Hilda has a gun,' Molly added.

Adam just shook his head.

'What?' Abigail demanded.

'I don't think she is a suspect.'

'Why not?

'Tell us!'

Adam hesitated. Molly and Abigail stood directly in front of him on the footpath, stopping his progress and challenging him to answer. 'I made a fool of myself,' he said bitterly.

'Why? What have you done?'

Adam told them. He had decided that he would test Hilda Pritt to see if she really was a genuine pilot. So he had devised some questions about aircraft which would show if she knew what she was talking about. Then, in a long chat with her, he slipped these questions in. 'I thought I was being really clever,' he said.

'When?' asked Molly.

'When you'd been sent to bed.'

'What sort of questions?'

'Well, I asked her if a Spitfire was slow at take-off when it had a full load of bombs.'

There was a brief silence. 'What's wrong with that?' Abigail asked.

'A Spitfire's a fighter,' Molly said. 'It doesn't *have* bombs.'

'Oh.'

'What other things did you ask?'

It was too embarrassing for Adam to explain. 'It doesn't matter what they were,' he said. 'She got them all right.'

'So she really is an ATA pilot?'

'I even tried to tempt her into telling a lie. I knew that those women pilots aren't allowed to fly bombers, so I asked her a question about Whitleys.'

'What's one of them?' Abigail asked.

'Armstrong Whitworth Whitley. It's a bomber. But she didn't try to bluff her way out of it. She was quite honest. She just admitted she'd never flown one.'

'Just because she's a pilot doesn't mean she can't be the murderer.' Abigail said.

'Except the ATA only posted her here after the

murder,' Molly pointed out, remembering the day Hilda had arrived.

'So,' Abigail said, 'we can eliminate her from our enquiries.'

'She must have thought I was mad.'

'Or up to something,' Abigail said helpfully.

Adam *had* been up to something – which was probably why he snapped at her. There was no talking to him that day.

At the Ely Guesthouse, Adam sat down after tea and began to draw. Molly was reading and at first took little notice. But later she glanced across to see what he was doing. He was making a copy of the stolen painting, Pissarro's *Vue de Pontoise*.

Why was he doing that? Adam raised his head and looked into Molly's eyes. For a moment she thought it was a challenge. Then she realised that he was completely unaware of her.

At that moment, Cuffey also saw the drawing. He stared at it for a minute, looking puzzled.

Then he looked at Adam. 'That . . .' he said. He looked again, puzzlement changing to astonishment. 'It's . . . '

Adam returned to reality. 'It's a copy,' he said. 'It's a painting by Pissarro.'

'Dear boy, I know it's a copy. But do you mean to say that you remember it so well that you can . . . ' It seemed so impossible to Cuffey that he couldn't finish his sentence. 'How did you do that?'

'Oh, I just remember it. I saw it in the paper.'

'Do you mean to tell us that you did it entirely from memory?' Cuffey's voice was hushed. Molly could see that he was shaken.

'Yes,' Adam said.

'But when . . . ?'

'It was in the paper. The *Daily Express*. It was about the painting being stolen. And there was a picture of it.'

'Dear boy, you must be a genius! That was weeks ago!'

'It's also in one of my art books.'

Cuffey and Mrs Barnes looked at one another in disbelief. Molly could see that her mum thought there was something odd about all this. She hated lying – and she thought there was lying going on here.

'Adam, did you really draw that from memory?'

Adam glanced at Molly. 'Yes,' he said.

It was true, Molly thought. But not quite true in the way her mum thought it was.

'I wouldn't have thought such a thing was possible,' Cuffey muttered.

For the next hour, there was an unpleasant atmosphere in the living-room. Mrs Barnes had the wireless on and sat close to it, listening to Mr Priestley's *Postscript* on the Home Service. Cuffey read his newspaper but he seemed restless and preoccupied. Adam sat at the table, scribbling something in his sketchbook. Molly tried to read, but the tension in the room made her uncomfortable and she couldn't concentrate.

Some time later, Adam pushed his sketchbook matter-of-factly across the table towards Cuffey and Mrs Barnes. They stared at it, and Molly moved round so that she could see too.

What Adam had drawn this time was an almost faultless black-and-white pencil copy of the *Mona Lisa*.

Before any of them could say anything, Adam went out and they heard him open the door that led into the back yard. A few moments later Molly joined him.

Molly felt desperately sorry for him, though she was not sure why. They stood side by side, looking up to the sky. No enemy aircraft. No clouds either. Adam looked at Molly's profile, shadowy in the moonlight. Her head was raised, her hair hung back, and her throat and face were clearly outlined. The previous night, she had seemed like a two-year-old in a tantrum. Now she might have been a queen from an old story about King Arthur, remote and beautiful.

Adam was arrested, absorbed. He forgot all about Pissarro.

It was Cuffey's turn to be tested. When Abigail heard how Adam had questioned Hilda Pritt, she made up her mind that Cuffey had to be cross-examined too.

Abigail would never have dreamed of talking to Cuffey about his girlfriends or what he was like as a little boy. But she did like him. And she was unlikely to forget that he had probably saved her life. It was a long drop from the roof of Paradise Barn.

However, he *was* on their list of suspects. So, when she arrived at Molly's house to find him sitting alone with a map spread out on the big kitchen table, she took her chance. Hilda was in her room upstairs, Cuffey told her, and Mrs Barnes had taken Molly to get a new pair of shoes.

'Molly said you were to wait,' Cuffey said. 'She'll only be about half-an-hour.'

So Abigail sat at the table beside him and looked at the map he had been studying.

'Is this to do with your work?'

'Yes. It's a map of Great Deeping and the area around it.'

Abigail had seen that at once. 'Do you work for the War Department?' she asked.

Cuffey looked a little surprised. But he answered her question. 'Yes, in a way. I am advising them.'

'Advising them about what? Are you a sort of soldier?' Unlike Adam, Abigail had not prepared her questions in advance.

'Well, for many years I worked as a road engineer.'

Abigail frowned, not understanding.

'I designed road-bridges, mostly. And level-crossings. And I worked on a couple of road-tunnels. In France, mostly.'

'In France?'

Aha! Abigail thought. *France!*

'And in this country too.' Cuffey was smiling at her.

Abigail brightened up. 'Did you design *our* level-crossing?'

'No, that was built seventy or eighty years ago. By the Victorians.'

'Why does the War Department want to know about bridges and level-crossings?'

'If the enemy invade, they will have to drive their lorries and tanks and guns along our roads. Or put them onto trains. The easiest way to stop that is to blow up the bridges and crossings.'

Abigail had seen trains loaded with tanks passing through Great Deeping, mostly at night. But they had been British armaments, not German.

'Are you planning to blow up *our* level-crossing?'

'I doubt it. In this part of England, it's the bridges we would go for.'

'I still don't understand . . . '

Cuffey turned away from the map on the table so that he could explain to Abigail. 'What the War Department needs to know,' he said patiently, 'is where, exactly, the explosives need to be put under a bridge to make sure it is destroyed at the first attempt. There won't be time to hang around placing a second lot of explosives.'

Abigail had lost sight of the purpose of her questioning. Her level-crossing had *always* been there. Everything in her life had grown up around it.

'But how would we know if you were going to blow it up?'

'It wouldn't be me,' Cuffey said. 'I know nothing about bombs. What I know about is the structure of bridges. Placing explosives isn't my job.'

'Yes, I *know*. But how would everybody know someone was going to blow up all those places? Someone on a bike might be crossing one of the bridges just as it gets blown up!'

Cuffey smiled. 'That wouldn't happen, Abigail. And, besides, if the Germans really do invade us, everyone will know.'

'How?'

'Well, to begin with, the church bells would be rung all over the country. Everyone would know what that meant.'

'Like they did in September,' Abigail said. The memory of that evening sent goose-pimples along her arms. 'But that was a false alarm,' she added.

'Yes,' Cuffey said. 'It worked though, didn't it?'

Abigail nodded thoughtfully.

'The sound of those bells coming across the fields from your church was enough to give everyone the creeps,' Cuffey said.

'It isn't my church,' Abigail said. 'I'm chapel.' She felt that her cross-examination of Cuffey was getting nowhere. She looked again at the map. 'Which ones are going to be blown up, then?' she said.

Cuffey smiled. 'I'm afraid I'm not allowed to tell you that.'

Abigail did not respond. She was seriously troubled.

'Abigail, listen.' She studied his face, concentrating, wanting reassurance. 'The Germans have left it too late. The winter's coming. They should have invaded when the weather was good and the days were long. It's probably not going to happen at all.'

'They might come next spring.'

'True. But by next spring everything might have changed.'

Abigail heard Molly's voice outside. 'Mum! They *pinch!*'

That evening the girls decided that Charlie Leggett should be told about his missing shovel. Adam went with them because they were nervous.

'We found it in Paradise Barn,' Abigail explained.

'In the *barn*? How did that git *there*?' Charlie said. He stared and stared, as if he wanted to eat them with his eyes.

'We found it there,' Molly said.

'How did you come to find it?'

'We were rootling about, and we found it,' Abigail said. 'We've left it just inside the door for you. You can go and get it whenever you like.'

'Then you can dig your garden,' Adam said helpfully.

They all looked at Adam disapprovingly. 'What?' he demanded.

'You don't dig with a shovel,' Abigail said.

'What do you do with it then?'

Charlie Leggett, as if talking to an idiot, said: 'You *dig* with a *spade*, and you *shovel* with a *shovel*!'

Adam nodded slowly, understanding the distinction. But Charlie was already thinking about something else. 'Tha's historical, y'know. My old shovel . . .'

Monday 4th November ~ after school

The three of them came into the kitchen after school on Monday afternoon to find Mrs Barnes and Cuffey talking to Sergeant Bly. The three grown-ups turned to face the three children.

'There you are!' Mrs Barnes said. 'Sergeant Bly needs a word with you.'

Molly watched her mum's face anxiously. There was seriousness there, certainly, but no sign of disapproval. There was a lot of disapproval these days.

Michael Bly explained. 'It's about the caravans in Bunty Fen,' he said. 'You know the ones I mean? I want you to promise to stay away from them.'

After only the slightest pause, Abigail said, 'Why us?'

The Sergeant smiled. 'Because you and Molly used to help clean them before the War, didn't you?'

Does he know everything we do? Molly wondered.

'Last night, they were smashed up.'

'Smashed up?' Cuffey said. He looked worried and anxious.

'Well, to be precise, someone found the keys and went into every one of them. They didn't exactly smash them to bits – I shouldn't have said that. But whoever it was went pretty wild. They seemed to be looking for something.'

'How did they get in?' Mrs Barnes asked.

'They found the keys. Mr Spinks had left them in the office. But the odd thing is . . . '

All three of the children knew what the odd thing was.

' . . . we found the key-ring in the grass. But one of the keys has gone missing. So the intruder had to smash a window to get into one of them.'

Molly – for the briefest second – remembered the taste of dusty rain on her tongue.

The policeman turned back to Mrs Barnes. 'We don't know where the missing key is. Nor why it went missing. Mr Spinks is sure it was on the ring with all the others.'

Molly knew where the caravan key was. So did Adam. It was in Molly's bedroom, at the bottom of an old jewellery box her Auntie Phyllis had given her.

'Anyway, the point is,' the policeman said, 'you mustn't be tempted to go anywhere near those caravans.'

They promised they wouldn't.

'Is it anything to do with the murder?' Mrs Barnes asked.

Sergeant Bly hesitated. 'Well, we think it might be,' he said. 'The intruder seems to have been quite violent.'

There was a persistent worry inside Molly's head. In the middle of arithmetic, half-way through a game of hop-scotch, in the quiet hours of the night, this worry would come forward to the front of her mind. She knew what it was – they were in possession of a famous stolen painting and neither Adam nor Abigail seemed to understand the enormity of it. *We'll hand it in,* they said – *soon*. But when was *soon*? Molly wanted to know.

And the paint-box – *that* had been stolen too and was now hidden upstairs under Adam's mattress.

Something else troubled her. An awareness of danger, almost a *smell* of encroaching menace. The murder had started it. And the hand-gun in Hilda Pritt's bag was part of it. So was the big American they had seen searching the barn.

Now someone – probably the American again – had broken into the caravans.

Afterwards, Abigail said, 'We were very clever.'

'Why?'

'At school,' Abigail continued, 'when one of the teachers blames the whole class for something, the people who've done it always look at each other. I've noticed.'

Adam agreed. 'I expect teachers are trained to watch for it.'

'Well, *we* didn't,' Abigail said. 'When he mentioned the missing key, we didn't give ourselves away.'

Adam moodily kicked a stone along the street ahead of them.

'We're getting very good at being bad,' Molly said sadly.

Wednesday 6th November ~ after school

The Ely Guesthouse was very quiet that Wednesday afternoon.

Mrs Barnes had taken Baby William to visit a friend at the other end of the town. Molly and Abigail had gone to Paradise Barn – usually they all went, but Adam had a new picture in his mind that he wanted to make a start on. So after school he went straight home and settled himself to work at the kitchen table.

Cuffey was upstairs, he thought. Hilda Pritt was moving about in her room and he could hear the Ascot heater roaring softly. One of them was running a bath.

The stillness of the afternoon was interrupted by the wailing of the air-raid siren. All thoughts of drawing vanished from Adam's mind. This was an unusual time for an air-raid. He raced outside to look for the approaching bombers but there were none in sight. He could hear them clearly – a distant heavy rumble, like an approaching thunderstorm.

But instead of growing louder as the planes drew near, the sound remained at the same volume. He could hear bombs exploding and the sharp muffled thuds of anti-aircraft guns. This was different, more like what happened over London. Here, the planes usually flew straight over on their way to the Midlands. It was the same when they flew back, except that they sometimes jettisoned any remaining bombs.

Adam tore back into the house and raced upstairs to his room for a better view. On the landing he found himself face-to-face with Hilda Pritt, draped from her shoulders to her knees in a pink towel.

'There's a raid, Miss!' Adam said breathlessly.

'Of course there is!' she said coolly. 'I am about to have my bath – so it was *inevitable* that there would be a bloomin' raid! You should get into the shelter.'

'What about you?'

'I'm having my bath,' Hilda said. 'It's jolly ages since I enjoyed a long soak and I'm not going to be prevented a moment longer.'

She was either brave or foolish. Adam gave no thought to it – but he had no intention of going to the shelter. He raced into his room. From his window he had an imperfect view, obscured by the roofs of the town. But he could see enough to know what was happening. A few miles to the north-east of Great Deeping, the Germans were bombing the airfield. He estimated that there were about twenty bombers. They had passed over once and were circling back for a second attack. There were fighters above them and among them, both British and German, Adam supposed. But they were too far away and he couldn't be certain.

One of the bombers had become separated from its

squadron. It was heading towards Great Deeping and losing height. A Junkers 88. As it drew nearer, Adam could see the crosses on its wings and fuselage, and the swastika on its tail section. A faint pale wisp of smoke came from somewhere close to the rear of the plane. It had been hit. Two British fighters were in pursuit. Hurricanes.

Adam – who had seen it happen before – knew exactly what was going to happen.

Molly and Abigail had no special reason for going to Paradise Barn that day. Lately, it had become an after-school habit, usually with Adam there too. They always checked that the Pissarro was still safe, a daily ritual. Then they messed around for half-an-hour or so before going home as darkness fell.

When they heard the air-raid warning they knew what they had to do. They had to run either to Molly's house or to Abigail's and get safely into a shelter. But when they went outside the barn, they knew at once that this was unlike the other raids. There were no aircraft passing overhead. Instead there was a prolonged distant roar.

Then they saw that one plane was heading straight for them, flying low over the town. They knew it was an enemy bomber and two British fighters were chasing it.

Abigail realised immediately that there was no time to get to a shelter. She knew that people caught outside during a raid were sometimes machine-gunned by enemy planes. 'Quick! Inside!' she shouted.

Molly dithered. So Abigail grabbed her and dragged her bodily back inside the barn.

'We'll get under the tractor,' Abigail said. And before Molly had fully understood why, Abigail had got them both installed under one of the ancient pieces of farmyard equipment that lived in the barn.

The noise in the sky intensified – and then changed as the German plane banked in a different direction.

Adam had known exactly what was going to happen – and he was proved right. In order to gain height, the Junkers would have to dump its remaining bombs.

The German bomber had approached the town from the north, flying almost exactly along the line of the High Street, and directly towards the Ely Guesthouse. It was so low that it looked as if it must crash into the roof-tops at any minute.

But Adam never took his eyes off it as it flew closer. He saw the bomb-doors open under its wings, and several sticks of bombs were jettisoned. They swung jerkily beneath the plane as they fell, moving at first almost at the same speed. He lost sight of them almost at once and then came the explosions, a tumultuous succession of blasts that shook the house and rattled the windows.

Right in the middle of the town, he thought. The

plane was heading directly towards him, growing larger and darker. But there were no more bombs. Adam instinctively ducked as it roared across the street outside, and over the roof of the guesthouse. Every window-pane shook, every ill-fitting door rattled. Somewhere, a terrified cat hissed.

Adam raced out of his room, along the landing and into Molly's room, so that he could see the sky at the front of the house. The Junkers came into sight immediately. It was successfully gaining height, rising in a wide curve away from the town.

Immediately one of the two Hurricanes came into view. There was a burst of gunfire. More smoke poured from the Junkers, and then, briefly, flames. One of the plane's wings broke free and fell off, and the rest of the aircraft spiralled wildly downwards. A small black object seemed to fall free, then the plane exploded as it hit the ground. A black cloud of smoke drifted away into non-existence.

From a neighbouring house, Adam heard someone call out: 'They've got the bastard!'

A parachute blossomed with a figure swinging below it. One of the crew had escaped.

The Hurricane swooped triumphantly upwards. Much higher, its companion was circling. Adam saw both planes waggle their wings briefly in greeting. Then they curved back to rejoin the fight above the airfield and within minutes everywhere was quiet and all noise seemed to be at a distance.

Adam had gripped the curtains of Molly's bedroom window so hard that he'd pulled one end of the curtain-rail away from the wall. He was enthralled, excited, scared.

The parachute drop was a short one. The airman landed and Adam could see him freeing himself from the harness. He staggered a little, as if drunk. Then he set off slowly across the field towards the nearest building.

Paradise Barn.

Molly had heard the roar of the German bomber growing louder as it crossed the town – and she wanted to see. What was the point of cowering in the shadows like a couple of frightened dormice?

'Come on!' she said. 'We'll feel less scared if we know what's going on.'

Abigail was not so sure. As they were walking back towards the open doorway of the barn, they heard the explosions. For a second they gazed at each other in appalled amazement. Then they rushed to look – in time to see huge dark clouds rising from the centre of the town and turning a sinister rosy pink in the low light of the setting sun.

Then came the bomber, almost directly overhead, and a British plane in pursuit.

Disintegration, death and escape, they saw it all. Two or three bits of shrapnel hit the roof of the barn, rolling and rattling down the tiles, then thudding softly into the ground. There was a strong smell of petrol.

Before they had fully grasped what they had seen, the German was walking across the fields straight towards them.

'I'm going to wet myself,' Abigail whispered. 'Oh, please, God . . .'

She picked up an old bit of machinery, a rusty metal bar, as if it could somehow save their lives.

'Miss Pritt! Miss Pritt!'

Hilda Pritt shouted from the bathroom. 'What is it?' Then, less loudly, to herself, 'Is there never to be any peace?'

'A Junkers 88! It's crashed!'

'I'm delighted to hear it.'

'But the pilot! He's escaped. He got out.'

'Bully for him!'

'But he's wandering about in the fields!'

'Then go and capture him. Take him in.'

'*What?*'

'He won't put up any resistance.'

'But I . . . '

'For God's sake leave me in peace! I haven't enjoyed a hot bath for *ages*! If you think I am going to get out and chase all over muddy fields . . . '

Adam knew there was no bolt on the bathroom door. It was the rule in the guesthouse that if the door was shut you didn't go in – and for a moment he thought he might rush straight in, pull the bath-plug out and *force* Hilda Pritt to do something.

But he had a better idea. He raced into her bedroom, casting his eyes around for her shoulder-bag.

Molly and Abigail hurriedly scanned the barn for somewhere to hide. Plenty of places for small objects, such as paintings or shovels. Plenty of places for sheltering under. But there wasn't time – the German was already close. They backed away from the door as they heard him approaching outside. He walked in, and saw them at once.

He stopped, facing Abigail and Molly. 'I am Oberleutnant Hans Lange,' he said. 'Take me to the Royal Air Force.'

His voice struck terror into their hearts. It was high, metallic, as if it was used to uttering terrible cruelties. His face was angular and pale, his mouth tight and square, his features sharp and pinched. And he stood stiffly, looking down at them with an unblinking fixed glare.

The metal bar fell from Abigail's hand and clattered on the brick floor.

Adam appeared behind him, silhouetted sharply against the late afternoon sunlight. They saw him taking in the situation. He saw the two girls, backing away, scared, from the man who was threatening them.

He did not hesitate. 'Put your hands up!' Adam snapped.

Oberleutnant Lange swung round angrily. 'My God! The British must be terrified of us if they are arming their children!'

With his eyes on the gun which Adam was holding, he slowly raised his hands above his head. 'I am Oberleutnant Hans Lange,' he said again. 'You must take me to the Royal Air Force.'

When the Junkers 88 had flown over the rooftops of the town, Cuffey had been in the guesthouse all the time, quietly working in his room. He had toyed lazily with the idea of going downstairs to the kitchen and crawling into the shelter. But when the aircraft jettisoned its bomb-load over the town he rushed to his window to see.

His bedroom faced up the length of the High Street, and he saw at once that the centre of the town had been hit. Quickly he began to put on his shoes so that he could go and see what had happened. But then he heard someone rushing about from room to room, and a moment or two later he heard Adam and Miss Pritt shouting at one another through the bathroom door. He could not distinguish the words, but he caught something about capturing a prisoner.

He heard Adam slam the back door as he rushed out. Cuffey hurried into one of the front bedrooms and stared across the fields behind the town. He saw a small figure staggering across the fields towards the old barn that the children spent so much time in. Smoke was rising from the crumpled wreckage of the plane.

Cuffey set off in pursuit of Adam. When he came to the end of Dead Man's Way he could see the boy ahead, with a pistol in his hand. He was racing at a speed that the older man couldn't hope to match. But he went doggedly on, gasping and clutching his side.

As he reached the end of the footpath and turned onto the farm-track that led to the barn, he saw the airman go into it. A couple of minutes later, he saw Adam stop outside the doorway, peer cautiously in, and slowly walk inside with the gun held firmly.

'I'm taking you prisoner,' Adam said. As far as the girls could see, he was totally unafraid.

'Yes. Who are you, please? You must take me to the Royal Air Force.'

Adam had no idea how to take the prisoner to the RAF. What was he to do?

'*At once!*'

Molly and Abigail, clutching one another, saw Cuffey come into the barn behind Adam.

'Cuffey!' one of them cried. They hurried eagerly around the German pilot to be with Adam and Cuffey, just inside the door of the barn.

Cuffey was gasping for breath. But he managed to

speak. 'Give me the gun,' he said quietly.

'No!' Adam said. 'He's a Nazi! He's dangerous!'

'So is that gun.'

The airman said something in German. 'Deutschland siegt an allen fronten!'

Then Cuffey spoke in German and the airman replied, eager, relieved. Molly and Abigail were startled and confused. They had never heard German spoken, except in films.

'Why . . . ?' Molly began to ask. She was looking into his face, confused.

Cuffey opened his arms and stooped down to their level, with Adam on one side and the girls on the other.

'He might kill us,' Molly said.

In a low voice, which the German would hardly have been able to hear, Cuffey spoke to them. 'He's not dangerous. Look at him! He's *frightened*! He's not much more than a boy.'

Frightened? How could he be frightened? He's a *Nazi*!

And yet . . .

'Look at his hands. His legs. His face.'

They looked. The young German's hands were clenched tight, his legs were trembling, his face was white and strained.

'But what's he got to be scared of, now that he's on the ground?'

'Abigail, *think!* He has just lost the rest of his crew.

They're dead. He has survived by the skin of his teeth.'

'All the same,' Abigail began to say.

' . . . And he probably thinks he will be taken away and shot.'

All three of them protested at that. How could Cuffey think that?

But Cuffey persisted. 'He doesn't know what's going to happen to him. He has probably been told that we shoot prisoners-of-war.'

Cuffey stood up. 'Keep your hands above your head,' he said to the prisoner in English. To Adam he said, 'Put the gun away.'

'But . . . '

'He won't be any trouble. And I don't think Miss Pritt would want everyone in Great Deeping to know about her gun.'

They left Paradise Barn in procession, out into the chilly air.

'Why hasn't one of the Air Raid Wardens come?' Molly said. 'They must have seen him bale out from their post on the church tower.'

'They've had other things to do, Molly,' Cuffey said. 'There have been bombs in the middle of the town.'

Privately, Cuffey thought the church might have copped it. Wardens and all.

They entered the town through Lower Lane. In the outer streets, there was silence everywhere, as if someone had switched off the sound. And there were no people – no-one walking home from the shops, no-one in the houses, no-one closing their shutters for the night.

The sky was quiet too. There were no more sounds of aircraft in the distance. A few miles to the east, where the airfield was, several huge plumes of smoke billowed silently upwards.

In the High Street there was a different kind of strangeness. Almost the entire population of the town had been drawn to see the damage done by the bombing. People talked quietly to one another as they stood and looked at the wreckage. Women, children, old men – and a few frantic Air Raid Wardens. Babies were carried, toddlers were lifted up so that they could see, old men pointed with their walking-sticks. Sergeant Bly was there, and some firemen and Red Cross women. Orders were being given, and suggestions being made – all in subdued voices.

Oberleutnant Lange had piloted his failing plane along the length of the High Street and most of the bombs had landed precisely in the middle of the road. About a quarter of a mile of the street was now a succession of deep uneven craters with rubble blasted on all sides. Thick flat pieces of tarmac lay at all angles, some of them tilted on the edges of the craters. Streetlights and telegraph poles lay flat, or leaned at unnatural angles. There were broken pipes, one of them pouring out a stream of brown water. The buildings on each side of the street still stood, but their windows and shop-fronts had been destroyed. There was broken glass everywhere.

Mr Woodruff's toyshop had come off worse than the others. One of the bombs had fallen off-centre and had hit the frontage of his building. Hundreds of toys had been blasted into the street and lay scattered among the débris. A big brass till lay on its side.

Not all of the bombs had landed in the street. The Crown Inn was no longer there. There was a hole in the town, and an unfamiliar view of neighbouring walls and rooftops looking bare and exposed – and a bit of sky that had been shut out since the inn had been built in 1609. People stood staring at the mountain of smashed bricks and tiles, and the tangle of wooden beams. Some of them were burning, bright yellow and orange in the failing light.

The streetlight, the post-box, the telegraph pole and the bus-shelter that had once stood at the road-junction were either buried or destroyed. There was dust everywhere.

No-one had been killed. The three guests who had been in the hotel had all taken refuge in the Anderson shelter in the back-yard. They were bruised and covered in dust, but safe. The five women who worked at the hotel had hurried into the big shelter in the playground of the infants' school on the opposite side of the street. The railings at the front of the school had been blown flat, but otherwise the school was undamaged.

People moved as if they were under a spell. As Cuffey and Oberleutnant Lange approached, followed by the three children, the crowds backed away and stared in silence.

Oberleutnant Lange slowed slightly, and his body stiffened. Cuffey spoke to him in German.

Abigail caught the word *Hitler*. 'What did you say to him?' she demanded.

'I pointed out that this would not be a good moment to give the Hitler salute.'

As they picked their way among the rubble, people drew themselves back tightly, to stay clear of the German.

Someone in the crowd shouted: 'If you'd gone another half-a-mile, mate, you could have landed right in the middle of the POW camp. Saved us a bit of trouble!'

There was laughter. Not much, but enough to relieve the tension. Oberleutnant Lange didn't understand.

A soldier approached. He was a local man – Bobbie Burton's dad – who had just arrived home on leave. He had his .303 with him, but no rounds. He was embarrassed, but firm. 'Are you an officer?' he said to the German.

'Ja. I am Oberleutnant . . . '

Private Burton straightened to attention briefly and saluted the enemy officer. In response, Oberleutnant Lange shot his right arm out and up in the German salute. But he had the sense not to say *Heil Hitler*.

Mrs Lettie Greene came out of the post office, ignoring the broken glass at her feet. She was the post-mistress, a strict, efficient, rather humourless lady. Her husband had been killed in the First World War. She wore stiff brown tweed, skirt and jacket, and pinned at her chest were her husband's military medals.

She spoke to Cuffey. 'Bring him in here,' she said sharply.

They stopped, hesitating.

'He needs a cup of tea.'

Oberleutnant Lange looked confused.

'I must come too,' Bobbie's dad said.

Mrs Greene took the British soldier and the German prisoner into her house behind the post office. As she turned to close the door, she said to Cuffey, 'The guards at the camp will be here soon to collect him. I've phoned them.'

Slowly, the people were becoming active. The stunned silence was wearing off a little. Cuffey went over to help the ARP men, and Molly noticed that Hilda Pritt had turned up – in uniform – and was supporting an elderly man whose house was next door to the Crown. It appeared to be undamaged but he was scared that it might collapse at any minute.

Children were scavenging for Mr Woodruff's scattered toys, finding dolls, model cars and trucks, packets of coloured chalks, all manner of treasures. They were bringing their finds to Mr Woodruff. Already a system was being established: a table had been found, and a chair. Mr Woodruff – white-faced but cheerful – sat near one of the craters in the street receiving the recovered toys. Beside him, he had a big tin box full of glass marbles. Everyone who restored one of his toys was given a handful of marbles. One girl found a Hornby model level-crossing, complete with movable gates; she did better than the rest – she was given a tiny metal rocking-chair for a doll's house.

The scavenging quickly became a game, every child greedy to get a reward.

Molly saw that Abigail was talking animatedly to Adam. Adam was listening attentively. He nodded, and ran off back in the direction of the Ely Guesthouse.

Molly felt a sharp pang of exclusion. What had they been talking about, without her?

Further down Crown Lane, she saw her mother, standing with a group of people, looking harassed and worried. She worked her way over the fallen débris and joined her.

Mrs Barnes hardly seemed to notice. 'You're all right, then,' she said. 'What were you doing with that German?'

Molly wanted to begin telling her the long and complicated narrative of that afternoon. But it seemed impossible. Everyone was too preoccupied.

'I took him prisoner,' Molly said.

– Well, Abigail and me.'

– Adam was there too, later.'

– Then Cuffey came, and he did it really.'

'Oh, *Molly!* For heaven's sake! Where *were* you?'

'In the barn. We . . . '

'The barn! Why weren't you at home? You should have been in the shelter!'

'It was too late. It was safer to stay where we were.'

'I'm going to put a stop to you going to that barn!'

Molly despaired. 'Where's my brother?' she asked. She never called him *my brother*. What was the matter with her?

'I left him at Maggie Wilson's house when I heard the bombing. Molly, I want you to go and get him and take him home.'

Molly nodded sadly.

'And take him by the back way. You'll never get a pram along the High Street.'

'OK.'

'And, Molly, when you get home, change his nappy and peel some potatoes. Lots – about four times as many as usual.'

'Why?'

'Oh, *Molly!* Don't *fuss!* You're all muddle, as usual! The guests who were staying at the Crown are moving in with us. Where did you think they were going to stay?'

Molly hadn't thought about it at all. Adam was coming back, carrying something. Through the crowds of people milling about, Molly couldn't see clearly at first. Then she realised what it was – a large flat object. Adam handed it quickly to Abigail, who promptly –

along with all the other children – took it to Mr Woodruff's table.

Molly understood. Risky, she thought. Mr Woodruff might remember that it had been taken ages ago. But clever of Abigail to return it herself; if asked, she could truthfully say she hadn't stolen it.

But Mr Woodruff made no comment and Molly saw Abigail receive her reward in marbles.

One more stolen item returned to its owner, Molly thought. That only left the painting.

She approved. But she still felt left out. She knew with absolute certainty that Abigail was at that very moment thinking indignantly: *I should have got more than a few marbles for that!* She could almost hear her saying it.

'And, Molly,' said Mrs Barnes, 'keep the hood of the pram up – in case of falling shrapnel.'

There won't *be* any falling shrapnel, Molly thought crossly. It's already fallen. Inwardly she spoke to her mum – It's *you* who are in a muddle!

Then the church clock struck five. Slowly the strokes tolled out, and Molly listened, counting them. Had so much happened in just one-and-a-half hours? It seemed impossible. Time ought to have expanded along with drama. At half-past three, everyone in school had trooped out into the sunshine as they did every day – and had that been only an hour-and-a-half ago?

She crossed the road and stepped over the fallen railings. Across the infants' playground and round to the back of the school. Through a small gate that led into Church Lane. Across the lane, into the church-yard. She wanted to know that the church was safe.

Inside, it was almost dark. Molly stood quietly by the font. She could see that some of the glass of one window had been blown in. There was no other damage. Someone – some solitary church-lover, she couldn't see who – was stooping between the pews, brushing up the pieces. Molly could hear the tinkling of broken glass.

She turned to leave, glancing up to check that Adam and Eve were still safe. It was too dark to see clearly, but she could just recognise them there in the gloom.

The wicked old serpent still had his eye on everything.

Shadowy people were finding their way home in the black-out, and with them went Molly, pushing her baby brother in his pram.

She heard voices rising and falling as people told each other what had happened. Slow East Anglian voices, describing, grumbling, speculating about what the Germans would do next.

From a couple of fields away came the sound of a tractor in the darkness. Then the tractor fell suddenly silent and a voice came as clear as if the speaker had been on the other side of the hedge – 'Have to wait till daylight, I reckon.' Farmer Morton and a group of

Home Guardsmen were giving up the attempt to disentangle the bodies of the three German airmen from the wreckage of the bomber.

Molly wondered what they would do with the bodies when they found them. Or would there only be bits? Would there be a proper funeral? Supposing one man's leg got buried with another man's body – would it matter? Would their families get a message saying they were missing in action, feared dead? Like Abigail's mum?

The world had become full of cruel and sudden things. Yet people seemed to know exactly what to do and what to say. How did they manage to be so quick and crisp in what they did? Molly was amazed and envious.

The German airman had known exactly what to say. *I am Oberleutnant Lange. Take me to the Royal Air Force!*

Adam had known exactly what to do. So had Cuffey. He had understood at once. *He's not much more than a boy.*

Abigail too. When she'd seen the contents of Mr Woodruff's toyshop being returned to him, she immediately had her idea and told Adam what to do. It would have taken Molly hours even to think of it.

They were all so certain. Her mum as well, sorting out the visitors at the Crown. *Molly, you're all muddle, as usual!*

How can I help being muddled, Molly thought, when there are so many questions? They crowded in. How long would there be extra visitors at the Ely Guesthouse?

For a week? For the rest of the War? For ever? Would the Crown Hotel be re-built? Where would Marion Staines' granddad live now that his hotel had been bombed? Would Molly have to move into the little attic bedroom which she hated?

Had the cottage in Little Green been bombed? Had Hilda Pritt's granny been killed? And why had Hilda refused to come to their help?

The big question, though, was about Oberleutnant Lange. Molly wanted to believe that he was a generous enemy who had tried to jettison his bombs in the middle of the road where they would do least damage. But he might have aimed at the buildings and missed. Or been too scared to care.

How many people had he bombed since the War started? Was he a murderer? What about her own dad – had *he* killed people?

There was an inner voice which Molly was very familiar with; the conscience that told her when she had done wrong. But these questions came from somewhere else. This was not her conscience speaking. This was something else in her, dissatisfied and angry.

Why had Abigail and Adam plotted to return the paint-box without her?

Molly became aware that her baby brother was watching her from inside the depths of the pram, clutching the edge of the cover. He'd had a jerky ride and he had woken up and pulled himself into a sitting position. Molly felt ashamed, overcome with sudden affection. She spoke softly to him. He looked gravely into the dark world outside his hooded pram.

But it was a momentary distraction. The old question came back, the big overwhelming worry that was always there. What would people say when they found out about the stolen painting, the Pissarro? Would her mum write to her dad and tell him about it? Would there be a row? Would Molly have to go to prison? Or a borstal? Would it be in the papers?

Would the big American who had searched Paradise Barn be moving in with them now?

Oh, why couldn't the other two see that the painting must be handed in? *We'll think of a way of doing it so that we don't get into trouble,* they said. *Stop fussing!* they said. But they did nothing.

She manoeuvred the big pram through the kitchen door in the darkness. Inside, she felt her way to curtains and shutters before switching on the lights. She put a match to the fire laid ready in the grate, un-bundled Baby William from the pram, and turned herself into a housewife.

The nappy was disgusting but Molly dealt with it. She cleaned the nappy, Baby William's bottom, and her own hands. When it was all done, she sat him on the sink while she started on the vegetables. She gave him a potato and a blunt knife. 'You can help me,' she said to him.

There must be an end to this painting business, she

told herself as she worked at the sink. But Abigail will be angry.

Baby William reached for another potato and Molly saved him from falling head-first into the bowl of water.

She and Abigail had been best friends since before their memories started. Nevertheless, Molly had made up her mind. It had to be done.

It was only a matter of choosing her moment.

Saturday 9th November ~ evening

Finding the right moment wasn't easy.

At the Ely Guesthouse everything changed. Because of the increased number of guests, Mrs Barnes had re-opened the dining-room. There was a big mahogany dining-table, comfortable armchairs to curl up in, bookshelves full of books, and a wind-up gramophone with a brass horn and lots of 1930s records. It was Molly's favourite room and she was happy to light the fire every day.

The night the new guests arrived had been grim and muddled. But, after that, there was a cheerful atmosphere, especially in the evenings. The visiting Americans – always two of them, sometimes three or four – were interesting and funny. Mrs Barnes' rule was that the children should stay out of the room when guests were in it, but the Americans insisted that they liked to have the kids around.

There were a couple of night air-raids. The Americans came downstairs but refused to get into the shelter. They sat in the kitchen, drinking coffee. They joked and laughed while Molly and Adam lay under the table, listening, joining in sometimes, and exchanging conversation with American feet and American pyjama-legs.

In the evenings, Molly and Abigail shared one of the big armchairs. Adam usually sat at the table, drawing. Records were played on the gramophone and once or twice there was some dancing. One of the Americans could do card tricks. The three children watched with delighted concentration, determined to catch him out. But they never did, and they would sigh with pleased disappointment.

Cuffey sometimes joined them in the evenings but he was quiet in their presence. 'No, but they make me feel old,' he whispered to Molly when she asked him if he was unhappy.

Hilda Pritt was in her element, shining like a gaiety girl, performing, sparkling, flirting. Molly disapproved of it; Abigail studied it; Adam clung with difficulty to his vision of her as a fearless pilot.

'I'm *jolly* pleased the old hotel has been put out of action,' she declared. 'I know I shouldn't say it, but it's much more fun having you all here!'

' – There's no chance of getting bored with you chaps because you're never here for more than a couple of nights!

' – I *know*, darling! There, there! But it's lovely for me because as soon as one lot leaves a fresh supply arrives. It's a maiden's dream!

' – By the way, when is Rusty Steele due for another flight across the Atlantic?'

'Rusty's takin' some vacation, Hilda,' one of the pilots said.

Hilda, stretching an elegant leg and studying the turn of her ankle, said dreamily, 'How lucky you all are to be able to fly the Atlantic! I would just *adore* to do that!'

'It could probably be arranged,' one of the Americans said quietly.

Abigail and Molly sat very still. Adam stopped drawing. Something new had entered the conversation.

There was a pause. 'Are you serious?' Hilda said. Her voice was a husky whisper.

'It happens.'

Hilda stared at him, game for anything, her eyes wide with innocent mischief. 'Gosh!' she breathed.

'Why not? It's always possible to smuggle little objects in with the pilot.'

'Well, you may not have noticed, but I'm not exactly a *little object.*'

There was laughter, and someone made a joke about her being little in all the best places.

Molly and Abigail were all ears.

But Hilda persisted. 'Have *you* ever done it?'

'Well,' he said very slowly, 'I once took a bottle of Scotch home for my grandpapa.'

Well, Molly said inwardly, American-fashion, W*aall*. But she couldn't get it right.

When the laughter had quietened, Hilda persisted. 'But *big* stuff – have you ever taken anything . . .? *You* know what I mean.'

'I guess not,' was the careful reply. 'All I said was that it can be done.'

'Who?' Hilda was still the wide-eyed child, longing for some mischievous tit-bit of forbidden knowledge.

But none of them would say and there was a strange silence. Everyone was watching – Molly, Abigail, Cuffey, even Adam, and an elderly commercial traveller who had arrived that afternoon and was sitting quietly in the corner.

Hilda tried again. 'What about Rusty? Would *he* do it?'

'Well, he's due here on a flight in a few days. Then you can ask him.'

'When's he coming?' Cuffey asked.

'We don't know. We never do. The schedule is always being changed. But he's sure to come some day soon. Why? Do you know him?'

In her head, Molly repeated the word *schedule* American-wise, *skeddle, sheddle, skedule*.

'I've heard about him,' Cuffey said.

'There's a flight due tomorrow. He might be piloting that.'

'Are you on our side?' Molly asked the airmen. 'In the War?'

'We sure are, honey. We ain't declared War and we ain't doin' no fightin' right now. But we're sure as hell on your side!'

'America will be joining the War soon,' another of them said. 'You'll see.'

'I wish you would,' Molly said wistfully. 'Then we might win.' The thought of lots of young Americans – good-humoured and good-looking – coming over to join the fighting was cheering.

'If the enemy commits an act of aggression on the United States, we'll sure join in!'

'They bombed the hotel you were in,' Abigail said. 'That was an act of aggression.'

Everyone laughed. 'It sure was, kid! But I don't think the President is going to declare War because some crazy German pilot dropped bombs on the Crown Hotel in your little city.'

City? Molly thought.

'How's about a game of *Snakes and Ladders*?' one of them said.

Why did Cuffey look so miserable? Molly wondered. Normally, she would have talked to Abigail about it. But there was a quarrel going on between her and Abigail, a subterranean quarrel with no visible signs, because they still hadn't handed in the stolen painting. Abigail seemed unaware of it and there was no outward change in anything the two of them did. They still spent just as much time together, sometimes with Adam, sometimes not.

So Molly said nothing to Abigail about Cuffey. And, when he told her that he was going away for a few days, she thought: *that's* why he's miserable.

'When are you coming back?' she said wistfully.

'Friday, probably. Perhaps sooner.'

Thursday 14ᵗʰ November ~ evening

So *that's* Rusty Steele, Adam thought.

He had arrived that afternoon, by taxi, with a swagger in his look and a boast in his smile. A tall man, strong and slow in his movements, looking round with lazy interest at the unfamiliar guesthouse.

They'd seen him before.

He was the man they had seen searching the barn. Unmistakably. And, probably, he was the man who had ransacked the caravans. Molly was nervous. Illogically, because they'd had a close-up view of him through binoculars, she was afraid he would recognize them just as they recognized him.

Adam had a new project. He sat at the table in the dining-room, roughly mapping out a design for it. Mr Churchill, with cigar and hat, was in the top left-hand corner and out of his mouth came the words *THE NAZIS ARE COMING!* The middle foreground would have pictures of soldiers standing guard beside road-blocks. In the distance, a multitude of Heinkels and Messerschmitts approached, like a swarm of locusts. On the right-hand side, there was a close-up of Great

Deeping church tower, drawn so that you could see the bells swinging. From them came jagged zigzag lines with the words *BE PREPARED! THE NAZIS ARE COMING! TONIGHT!*

He would call it *September 7th.*

When the guesthouse visitors began to gather in the room for the evening, Adam took his sketch-book into the empty kitchen where he could concentrate properly. But the drawing wasn't going well. He couldn't capture the fear. So he gave up and went back to the dining-room.

He sat on the back of an old leather armchair, with his feet on its seat. It was his favourite perch when he wasn't drawing, and no-one seemed to mind. From his perch, he took everything in, methodically.

Abigail working at a jigsaw puzzle with a young American called Bud. Her long hair hung over her face, and was unconsciously hooked back every few minutes behind her ears. They talked sporadically – scraps of phrasing that sounded like a secret code. 'We need a bit of blue with some brown on the tip,' Adam heard Abigail say. 'Have you seen a bit of chimney-stack with a black patch?'

Mrs Barnes sitting beside the commercial traveller and talking quietly to him about the latest bombing in Birmingham.

Hilda sitting in a corner, chatting quietly to Rusty Steele, tossing back her head in a silent laugh, flinging back her hair, fluttering her hands up and down close to his arm, as if she was longing to touch him.

Low conversations everywhere. Everyone talking secrets.

Except Molly, who sat in Cuffey's usual armchair. She had a crumpled look, her body hunched and her eyes going miserably from one group to another.

Molly went upstairs to her bedroom to read her *Biggles* book.

When she came down about half-an-hour later, she could hear laughter in the dining-room. She stood in the passage for a moment, enveloped by silence. A soft, shadowy, familiar silence. Quietly in the dark she approached the kitchen.

At the door, she stopped and looked in. Rusty Steele was in there, alone, bending over the table. Adam had left his sketch-book there and the big American was looking at it, unhurriedly turning the pages.

As Molly watched, his attention was suddenly caught. He hadn't moved at all; yet Molly knew that something had arrested him.

It was Adam's pencil copy of the Pissarro painting.

Rusty Steele looked up thoughtfully. Molly watched him, intent and shameless, as he stared at the wall. But it was a mirror he was staring at – and she realised with a frightened start that he was thoughtfully watching her reflection as she stood in the doorway.

She slipped back into the shadows and fled silently along the passage to the dining-room. 'Why isn't Cuffey here?' she thought. 'Why did he have to go away just at this time?'

Friday 15th November ~ after school

'I think you'd better show me where it is,' Cuffey said.

When she arrived home after school on Friday, Molly had found Cuffey there. He'd said he would be back on Friday, and he was. So she wasted no time. She knocked on the door of his room, went in, and sat on the foot of his bed, facing him as he sat in his armchair.

He was surprised, of course – she had never done that before. But Molly hadn't hesitated.

The telling was easy, quickly done.

'This flower-press?' Cuffey said. 'Was it a *big* flower-press?'

Molly explained about Mrs Weathergreen's outsize flower-press.

'I think you'd better show me,' Cuffey said.

'Please don't be angry with me,' Molly said. 'Everyone else will be.'

Five minutes later, wrapped in overcoats and scarves, the two of them set off in the gathering darkness. Cuffey had his torch, but not switched on because of the black-out. It was dark and mizzly outside, though not raining. Molly took Cuffey's left arm; in his right hand he carried his flapping umbrella, using it like a walking-stick.

It dawned on Molly that it flapped about because it had lost the strip of elastic meant for furling it tightly.

They left the lane, climbed the stile, and set off along the footpath where the Frenchman had been murdered. It was narrow, and so Molly let go of Cuffey's arm and walked behind him. There was just enough remaining light – but only just – for them to see the path in front of them. Soon they reached the farm track which led to Paradise Barn.

Molly noticed that there was a pattern in the way Cuffey's umbrella moved. It came down to the ground almost exactly in time with his left foot. It never came down with his right foot. Sometimes he gave the brolly an odd little flourish in the air so that it missed coming down to the ground. But, every time, it resumed its rhythm and always met the ground in line with his left foot. Something to do with maths, Molly thought. You could make a rule about it.

The tip of the brolly made small round prints in the wet hard-packed mud. It was too dark for Molly to see them. But she could feel them in her mind, soft round stud-marks in the innocent ground.

When they drew near the looming blackness of the barn, Molly noticed that her heart was thumping hard in her chest.

Her body seemed to have understood the truth before her mind worked out what it meant.

Abigail sat, alone, in her mum's back room, bored and at a loss because Molly had not wanted her that afternoon.

Abigail did not nurse a sense of injustice. But she was unhappy. What was the use of Friday evenings if she had to spend them on her own?

On the table in front of her was a picture Adam had left behind. A rough outline for his planned illustration of the evening of September 7th.

Abigail remembered that September 7th was the night of the murder. So she found a pencil and drew in the corpse, lying on its back. It was only a rough copy – Adam wouldn't care. But Abigail was not good at drawing. The corpse she drew was a thick straight line with its nose and feet pointing to the sky. The nose was the same size as the feet. The feet were the same size as the church.

She looked out of the window. It was almost dark and time to close the shutters. In the gloom of the November twilight, she saw two figures making their way across the fields, one behind the other. A big person, and a smaller one. Cuffey and Molly, moving along the footpath towards Paradise Barn.

Abigail wondered what they could be doing. Should she follow them?

But at that moment Mrs Murfitt came in. 'Lay the table, Abigail,' she said. 'Tea's ready.'

Abigail opened a drawer for the table-cloth and gave up all thought of going out to see what Molly and Cuffey were up to.

Inside the barn, Molly watched Cuffey shut the big doors. He closed one fully – that was the easy one. The other was jammed and had always defeated the efforts of the children. But Cuffey was able to move it. With a noise that was both a shriek and a crunch he managed to push it almost shut. There it stopped.

Then he took out the torch and switched it on. He shone the beam around the big barn, from wall to wall, as if he expected to find the painting hanging there.

He turned back to Molly.

'It was you, wasn't it?' she said in a small voice.

'It was me who did what?' Cuffey said. He was smiling cautiously.

'You murdered that man.' It was hard to get the words out. She felt overwhelmed, betrayed by this man she had trusted.

Cuffey just stared at her, as if puzzled.

'You killed him,' she whispered. 'Then you came back to look for the painting.'

'Molly . . .'

He moved towards her but she drew back. 'I don't care about the painting. It's nothing! But you are a *murderer*.' She wanted to hurt him with the word.

Cuffey took a deep breath. He placed the torch carefully on the tyre of an ancient tractor. In its level light, he faced Molly.

'Yes,' he said. 'I am. And may God forgive me.'

'*I* won't forgive you!' The words had burst out. 'Why did you do it?'

Cuffey breathed out slowly – a long weary sigh, as if body and soul were settling into a deep, sad place. 'Molly,' he said, 'how can I make you understand? You're just a child, you know nothing about greed. We wanted to be rich. And to out-smart the Nazis.'

We? Who else had been involved?

'But mostly it was greed,' Cuffey said. 'It was certainly greed with Dufour.'

Dufour! So he and Dufour had been accomplices.

Outside, the darkness was complete and it was raining heavily. They were enclosed now in the cold wet night.

'It was the day the Germans entered Paris. Everything was strange that day. No-one in the streets, the whole place deserted. It was a ghost city. Even in the Louvre Museum, all the staff were tense, watching from windows for the arrival of the troops.'

Old habits die hard. Even now, Cuffey's story-telling brought Molly's imagination into action. She saw thousands of German soldiers goose-stepping their way through the empty streets of Paris, with tanks and armoured cars, in black-and-white as they were on the newsreels.

'We were able to walk in through one of the service doors at the back of the Museum. No-one saw us. There were no visitors, and no-one on duty in the galleries. We could hardly believe how easy it was. We were able to take the Pissarro. And another – a less famous painting which hung in the same room. We just walked in and took them. Our idea was to sell the small one straightaway to raise some money. But it was the Pissarro we really wanted.'

Molly stood stiffly, frowning a little. Was he ashamed? Afraid? Did he care at all? She had no grip on grown-up guilt.

Cuffey continued, oblivious. 'Dufour was an art-dealer. We went to another dealer in Paris, a friend of his. Dufour knew he sometimes bought stolen paintings. He gave us cash for the small painting. And then we set off with the other one. I had a little van and we travelled in that. The roads were full of frightened people running away. There was no going north or east – there were German battalions everywhere. So we headed west, towards the coast of Brittany.'

He hesitated. Then – 'Do I have to tell you all this, Molly?'

'Yes.' She spoke firmly but, really, she was at a loss, hopelessly adrift.

'How long until your mother gets home and finds you're not there?'

'She won't be in until half-past six,' she said. Then her heart jumped into her throat as she realised she shouldn't have told him that.

However, Cuffey just shrugged and went on with his story. 'Dufour knew a fisherman who would take us across the Channel by night, to England. For a large payment. We got to Brest safely, but the invading Germans were not far behind us. They swept across the country and arrived the day after we did.'

Out of the corner of her eye, Molly saw a small mouse running soundlessly across the floor. They had seen it before – or one of its relations. It stopped near Cuffey's feet, quivering, bewildered by bigness. Then it skidded away into the shadows.

'Then Dufour double-crossed me. He gave me away to the Gestapo.'

Cuffey stopped and looked up, frowning, baffled by betrayal, wanting Molly to understand. But Molly already knew about being baffled by betrayal.

'They came in the night and arrested me. Not him, just me. So he got away with the painting and I was expecting to be shot.'

'But you shot him instead.' Molly was brutal.

'It wasn't quite like that,' Cuffey said quietly. 'The Germans hadn't enough soldiers to guard people like me. So I managed to escape. I had to lie low for a few days, but eventually I managed to find a fisherman to bring me over to England. We landed on the south coast, and I made my way here.'

'Why here?'

'Because of our original plan. Dufour had arranged for an American pilot to fly the painting to America. Smuggle it out. He knew someone in Chicago who would pay a fortune for it. This pilot always stayed at the Crown Hotel in Great Deeping. The trouble was that his flights were irregular and you could never tell when he would show up. But I knew this was where Dufour would have to come.'

Rusty Steele, Molly thought.

'It was Rusty Steele.' I *knew* he was a bad person, Molly thought. 'The trouble was, I didn't know whether Rusty was in on the plan to get rid of me. I still don't know. I arrived here that evening, by train, and I saw Dufour crossing the fields at the edge of the town. I went to meet him.'

There was a slow ruthlessness in Cuffey's telling now. Molly had never noticed before how big he was. In the enveloping shadows of the barn, she stood facing him, like an abandoned urchin facing a huge shambling villain.

'He was terrified when he saw me. He waited until we were close, then he drew a gun. I started to talk to him but . . . Well, he fired and missed. Before he could fire again, I grabbed his arm and there was a fight. You can guess the rest.'

'So you didn't *mean* to kill him?' Her voice was thin.

'I meant to stop him from killing *me!*' Everywhere was the sound of water, miniature torrents of rain dribbling and gurgling from the roof of the barn. 'Of course, once he was dead, I couldn't make him tell me where he had hidden the painting. I don't know whether Rusty was in on the deal too, but he certainly doesn't know where the painting is – I'm sure of that. He's been searching for it as well.'

Another silence. Only the slow fearful pulse of time. And the two of them, watching each other.

'What are you going to do?' Cuffey said at last. While the story was being told, no-one had to decide what happened next.

Molly didn't know. 'You're wanted by the police,' she whispered.

'You have power of life and death over me,' Cuffey said to her softly.

Molly thought to herself that *he* had power of life and death over *her*. He was a man, she was a girl, he was grown up, she was a child. She didn't feel powerful at all.

A damp gust of wind blew in through the half-open door, then subsided, as if the big barn were breathing. Molly stood like a rock, stern and unyielding. Inwardly, she was confused and frightened.

'Why didn't you tell me before?' she whispered.

He didn't hear, and leaned towards her, frowning.

Molly said it again, more loudly, sounding angry. And Cuffey straightened and shook his head hopelessly.

What am I to do? (Did she actually say this? Or did she just think it? Molly wasn't sure.)

'Spare me,' he said.

'The police will want . . . ' But her words petered out.

'Molly, if the police find out . . . '

'But you said you didn't *mean* to kill him. There was a fight and . . . '

He shook his head and raised his hand in front of her face, to stop her speaking. 'But I can't prove that. I doubt if they'll believe me. Especially as I'm a thief.'

Thoughts raced through Molly's mind like dogs chasing each other. Cuffey would come to no real harm if he gave himself up, she thought. They could go to the police station together. They could go past the guesthouse so that she could warn her mum that she'd be late back. Sergeant Bly was nice; he would be fair to Cuffey. But that other policeman! She wasn't so sure about him. Cuffey would be handcuffed and taken away.

Then a different thought came: she could let Cuffey escape now and tell the police later. And it wouldn't matter because by then he would have got away.

'They will hang me, Molly,' Cuffey said.

The mention of hanging resolved Molly. The tumultuous thoughts vanished in an instant and there were no more uncertainties. Whatever he had done, whatever he was guilty of, she would not allow Cuffey to be hanged. She had heard it on the six o' clock news often enough: *Tomorrow morning, at eight o' clock, the condemned man will be taken from his cell* . . . It had always made her feel ill, ruined the rest of the day, given her nightmares of sickness and shame. Perhaps she had an opinion on hanging after all?

Then she knew she was going to let him go. A final thought came into her head: *Cuffey is not a bad man. I know that for sure.*

'You must promise not to kill anyone else,' she said. But how foolish it sounded, she thought. How childish!

Cuffey said nothing. Was he reluctant to make such a promise? Or were there other possibilities waiting in the shadows of the barn? Other ways of dealing with this? Other outcomes? What was Cuffey thinking as he stood there facing her, with the painting he'd stolen concealed only a few feet away from him?

'You can get the five-past-seven to London,' she said to Cuffey. 'You've got time.' Her voice was severe, brisk.

Cuffey sighed. 'I will have to call in at the guesthouse and get my things,' he said.

'There is time for you to do that,' Molly said unhappily. Cuffey's sigh had been so deep that it seemed to take her with it.

There was a pause then, as if no-one quite knew how to end it. And it dawned on Molly that she would never see Cuffey again – and for something so final and so sad there ought to have been a sorrowful goodbye between them. On a dark railway platform perhaps, as they did it in films, with rain streaming down on them and steam from the engine swirling around their legs.

But nothing like that happened. And Cuffey didn't play his part properly. He should have thanked Molly for her generosity and left with dignity. But he didn't.

He spoiled his exit.

'I love that painting,' he said. 'I suppose there's no chance . . . '

'What?'

'You wouldn't let me . . . ?'

'What?'

'. . . have a look at it?'

Molly just shook her head slowly and emphatically. Cuffey sighed again, and looked around the barn. It was cavernous, filled with rubbish. There were a hundred hiding-places within its shadows.

Still Cuffey didn't move. 'You should tell the police about it,' he said. 'When I've gone. It'll be nothing but trouble to you if you don't.'

Molly wanted to distract his thoughts from the painting. 'Don't forget to pay your rent to my mum,' she said.

'It's paid,' Cuffey said sadly. 'It's paid in advance.'

'Well, you've got to pack your things when you get there. So you'd better get going if you're to catch that train.'

'Aren't you coming back with me?'

It was tempting. To walk home with him. But she shook her head. All that was over – she was angry with him, hurt. Frightened.

'I suppose not. Well, then . . . ' Cuffey moved towards the door. But he seemed unwilling to go.

They waited, both watchful. Was there, even now, some other way of ending this?

'You and Abigail must be careful with that man, Rusty Steele. I don't know him – but I think he is a very bad man.'

'Is he a murderer too?' Molly snapped.

'Not as far as I know,' Cuffey said, clearly stung by her words. 'But he was probably in league with Dufour. I am a more wicked man than he is, it's true. But be careful anyway. *Promise!*'

But Molly had done with making promises to Cuffey. So he turned towards the door. 'I'd better give you this torch,' he said.

'I've got one,' Molly said. Her voice sounded sharp and unfriendly. She took her torch out of her coat pocket.

'Oh,' he said. 'All right. I suppose I must . . . '

He turned towards the narrow door-space and was gone.

Molly went across to the door and listened intently. Then she put her head out and looked. Cuffey was out of sight. She could hear his footsteps slopping in the wet mud, fading into the darkness as he went.

She went back inside and found a small dark space behind some old boxes. They smelt faintly of onions. She huddled into it and hugged herself, pressing her chin onto her knees for comfort.

Her fading torch went out completely.

All through teatime, Adam's drawing lay on the table beside Abigail's plate.

Her mother rapped it with the back of a spoon. 'What's that supposed to be?' she said.

So Abigail tried to explain that it showed the Germans invading England on the evening of September 7th.

'But they didn't,' Mrs Murfitt said.

'Everyone thought they were going to,' Abigail pointed out.

'What's *that* then?'

'Oh, *I* drew that in. That's the murdered man.'

Mrs Murfitt eyed Abigail's bit of artwork. 'Not exactly Michelangelo, are you?'

'Can I have a second helping?'

'No more apple pie. Plenty of custard.'

So Abigail had a second helping just of custard. And, as she spooned it into her mouth, she was trying to capture a thought. A memory. Something Cuffey had once said to her.

Something about the sound of Great Deeping church bells giving him the creeps. Yes, that was it! So he *was* here that night, Abigail began to think. Yet he hadn't arrived until several days later. She remembered it clearly – she and Molly had met him in the street, loaded with luggage and looking for the Ely Guesthouse.

What did it mean? Abigail wondered. *And* he'd spent a good deal of time in France.

Her mother had gone out to the kitchen. Thoughtfully, Abigail licked the bowl clean of every last wipe of custard.

Molly shivered.

Now that she was alone in the barn, fear overwhelmed her. While Cuffey had been with her, it had been held back like a wild animal on a chain.

She was scared of the darkness. Scared to set off home. Scared to stay where she was. Scared that the mouse might run up her skirt. Scared that Cuffey might come back and search for the painting. Too scared to do anything. Scared that perhaps Rusty Steele might arrive and find her there.

Silly feverish thoughts gripped her. And still she crouched there, unable to move.

Then her ears caught the sound of something outside. Mostly, all that could be heard was the endless rain, softly pattering and dribbling as if it intended to drown the universe in an almost silent wetness. But, as she strained to listen, she distinguished a new sound. Squelching footsteps outside.

Molly shrunk herself tight and small.

Someone was in the doorway. A torch was switched on, its beam directed into the barn, sweeping this way and that.

Adam sat, drawing, at the table in the kitchen at the guesthouse. He was drawing a picture of Cuffey.

His teacher had given him a cigar-box full of broken fragments of charcoal. For several days, he had made sketches, getting used to its different feel and the different effects it gave him. He'd drawn the cat, a milkjug, a roofscape viewed from his bedroom window, and lots of trees.

When the back door was opened and Cuffey came in, Adam did not look up. People who knew they were being drawn always wanted to inspect. So Adam kept his head down over his work and hoped that Cuffey would show no interest.

But Cuffey just grunted a greeting and went straight through to the passage and upstairs to his room. After about ten minutes he came down again and went out.

Where's Molly got to? Adam wondered. But the part of his mind which had that thought was not engaged. He forgot about it and went on with his drawing.

'Molly?'

It was Abigail's voice.

'Where are you? Switch your torch on.'

Abigail! Lovely loyal Abigail!

Stiff and cramped, Molly released herself into a kneeling position. 'I'm over here. My battery's gone flat.'

Since the time they had dug up the bricks, there had been a candle, a candlestick and some matches left in the barn. Abigail found them, lit the candle and searched for Molly.

'What's happened? Tell me!'

Molly's eyes were dark-blue pools of unhappiness

and fear. She was shivering uncontrollably. 'Cuffey,' she said bleakly. 'He is the murderer. He killed that Frenchman.' She stared at Abigail, demanding a response.

So! Abigail thought. He *was* here that night! 'How do you know?'

Face to face, inches apart, they whispered in the candlelight.

'His umbrella made the marks in the mud. And – d'you remember? – it always flapped about. That was because it had lost its bit of elastic.'

'The knicker elastic!' Abigail said. A *murder*! It seemed too big, too important, for children to have to deal with.

That part of the story was easy for Molly to tell. Full of amazement but straightforward. But the rest – how she had accused Cuffey and raged at him, and how he had appealed to her not to let him be hanged – that didn't get told. Anyway, Molly couldn't remember exactly how it had happened. 'Then I let him go,' she said.

Let him go! Abigail thought. 'Molly!' she said firmly. 'You couldn't have stopped him.'

The candle-flame shivered sideways and the looming shadows in the barn leaned and swooped in lop-sided unison.

'I know,' Molly said.

'He could have . . . ' Abigail hesitated, then started again. 'He could have done anything.'

Molly nodded.

Abigail spoke in an appalled whisper as the truth sank in. 'You were shut in here with a murderer! Weren't you scared?'

Molly stared at Abigail as she worked it out. 'Only after he'd gone,' she said. And it was true.

'What are you going to do? You'll have to tell the police.'

But Molly shook her head.

'Molly, he's a *murderer*!'

They talked like this for some time, getting nowhere, kneeling on the cold brick floor, facing each other in the tiny candle-light.

'He's not a murderer!' Molly said tearfully. 'He's a man who killed someone. That's not the same.'

'It *is* the same!'

How could Molly explain what she meant? He had been a wicked man for – how long? – perhaps a minute. Did that make him wholly and fully a wicked man for the rest of his life? 'He's not a murderer,' she said weakly. 'He's Cuffey.'

'But he killed someone,' Abigail insisted.

'He wasn't a murderer when we first knew him,' Molly said. 'He wasn't a murderer until we knew he'd killed someone.' She knew what she meant but she could see that Abigail didn't.

Abigail – years older than Molly in some ways – could see that she was cold and frightened. 'Come on,' she said. 'Let's go home.'

Molly nodded and stood up. 'He was my . . . ' She didn't finish what she had been going to say. The sentence which had begun with words ended with tears. Molly's eyes flooded.

But Abigail knew what she'd meant. She was brisk. 'He can't be your best friend, Molly Barnes,' she said. '*I'm* your best friend!'

Molly squeezed her eyes shut tight to stop the crying that wanted to overflow.

'Cuffey's an old man,' Abigail said. 'You can't be best friends with an old man.'

'But he told me things. We talked about . . . ' Words failed Molly.

'I know,' Abigail said. 'But I've been your best friend since before the Battle of Hastings!'

Since before the Battle of Hastings was an old Abigail-joke. It cheered Molly a little. There were the beginnings of a weak smile. But half-hearted.

'We must go,' Abigail said. 'My torch is fading.'

It was true. The yellow-white light had been feeble from the start. It had already dulled to a pale grainy orange. And the candle would be no use to them outside.

'I'll get the painting,' Abigail said.

'Why?'

'He might wait outside till we've gone and then come back and search for it.'

'He wouldn't do that,' Molly said.

'He might. *I* would if it was me!'

In the end, though, they left the painting in its hiding-place. For Abigail, this was a purely practical decision: you probably shouldn't carry a valuable oil painting across muddy fields in heavy rain. They'd done it once before, but that time the painting had been safe inside the flower-press. And, anyway, where would they put it? Molly's thinking was different: she thought she knew that Cuffey would not come sneaking back for it. It would be a kind of test. She would like to *really* know.

'I can't tell Adam, can I?' Molly said. 'About Cuffey?'

'No,' Abigail said. 'Not if you're not going to tell anyone else.'

Then she had second thoughts. 'But we *did* tell him he could help us solve the murder. And he *has* helped.'

'I know. But I still can't.'

'Because he's a boy.'

'Because he's an artist.'

'Yes. He'd promise to keep the secret. Then he'd forget and put it in a picture.'

Molly thought Abigail was right. The things that were important to Adam were different.

'You'll get into terrible trouble – if you don't tell and they find out,' Abigail said.

Molly nodded. 'A murder!' she said. 'And I've *helped* the murderer. I'm a criminal, Abigail.'

'You're a successory,' Abigail said.

'A *what*?'

'Someone who helps a criminal.'

'You mean an *accessory*,' Molly said.

To Abigail, it still seemed worthwhile to try for a compromise. Fair to everyone, she thought. 'I tell you what! If you tell the police tomorrow, Cuffey will have had a whole night to get away in.'

But there was no response from Molly.

'Come on!' Abigail said. 'We'll go to my house and have some hot cocoa by the fire. My feet are frozen in these boots! Then we'll phone your mum and get her to send Adam round to fetch you home.'

Molly knew about Abigail's boots. They were two sizes too small and Abigail could get them on only without socks. Her feet would be painfully cold, and her toes cramped and crushed.

'There might be an air-raid,' she said.

Abigail blew out the candle. 'Too murky. The pilots wouldn't be able to see anything on a night like this.'

'They bombed Coventry last night, my Mum said. And it was murky then too.'

As they came to the door of the barn, Abigail's torch went out.

Just for a moment they stood together, frightened. Then they felt their way through the door, out of the dry darkness of the barn into the wet darkness outside. Rain was falling heavily. Clutching one another tightly like Siamese twins, they squelched and skidded into the night.

Saturday 16th November

The next morning was bright and sunny.

Abigail arrived early. 'Shall we go and see if the painting is still in the barn?' she whispered to Molly.

Molly didn't want to talk about it. 'Let's go outside,' she said.

'OK. But *are* you going to *tell*? About *Cuffey*?'

Abigail huddled close, persistent. Molly was evasive. She hadn't made up her mind yet, she muttered. And that was all she would say.

But Abigail was insistent. 'You don't have to go to the police,' she said. 'You can just tell your mum. She'll know what to do.'

'That would be worse!'

Abigail wouldn't leave the subject alone. 'What happened when you got home last night?'

What *had* happened? Molly had hardly given it much attention. But she remembered that her mum had said that Cuffey had had to leave unexpectedly. He'd left a note saying that he'd received orders from the government. Some urgent War business. 'I don't want you to be too upset, Molly,' she'd said. 'But I don't think he'll be coming back.'

Molly already knew that. 'Did he leave anything for me?' she'd asked her mum. 'A message or something?'

Mrs Barnes shook her head. 'No, love.'

Molly briefly told Abigail this. Without much interest, because it wasn't the real story. The real story couldn't be told because she had no clear words for it. It had to do with betrayal – and a deep, deep disappointment.

Abigail, however, was still in the world of practicalities. 'If you want to go to the police station, I'll come with you,' she said.

'Let's skip,' Molly said. 'It's ages since we skipped!'

Abigail realised it was no use. So they found Molly's old skipping-rope and skipped in the back garden. There ought to have been three people, but they looped one end of the rope over a stump on a laburnum tree. Molly held the other end and Abigail skipped.

'*Early* in the morning
At half-past eight,
We heard the postman
Knocking at the gate.
Up jumped Abigail
To open the door.
How many letters
Fell on the floor?
One, two, three . . .

Molly listlessly flicked the rope round. She felt as if she were trapped inside an inverted glass jar. She could see Abigail skipping away, she could see her house and the back garden. But the sun shone on her strangely and everything was at a distance, as if she didn't belong to it any more.

Adam came out of the back door, squinting in the low sunlight.

'Can you skip?' Abigail asked him breathlessly.

'No,' Adam said firmly. 'What's *she* up to?' He jerked his head towards the dining-room where the guests were still having breakfast.

The girls stopped skipping. 'Who?'

'Hilda! She's going on like mad about the flower-press.'

All three went indoors then, but Hilda had just left the room. There was no more talk about the flower-press but the three of them stayed anyway. Abigail and Adam kept a hopeful eye on the remaining sausages and bacon. Molly had no appetite.

Adam went with the girls to do the Saturday shopping that morning. It meant that their wages had to be divided into three instead of two, but the girls didn't mind as long as he was useful. He showed no interest in the shopping but he did as he was told.

The High Street was a street again. The rubble had been bulldozed into the craters and a steam-roller had spent an entire week flattening it hard. The volume of rubble that had come out of the ground almost exactly fitted the space that had been in the holes. Abigail commented on this fact, with amazement. Adam found it just as amazing that Abigail was surprised by it.

Molly wasn't interested.

There was no proper road surface, but it was flat and you could walk on it. Cycle wheels and pram wheels were difficult, and cars were not allowed at all.

But all the shops were open, except the toyshop. What was left of that had been boarded up. Mr Woodruff had moved his business into a disused room beside Jo Proudfoot's forge. It was an improvement in a way because it was closer to the school. Every day, schoolchildren lingered to watch the horses being shod; now they could look longingly at Mr Woodruff's toys as well.

Abigail had only one chance to speak to Molly when Adam was out of earshot. It was in the High Street, while he had gone into the chemist's for a bottle of aspirins.

'Well?'

Molly stared at her. 'I don't know yet,' she said. Abigail was beginning to irritate her.

But when Adam came back, Abigail made a suggestion which – briefly – startled Molly out of her gathering misery. 'Let's get rid of the painting, Molly,' she said. 'You were right all along. We should've taken it to the police ages ago.'

This cheered Molly a little. 'This afternoon?' she said. And Abigail nodded.

They looked at Adam, expecting disagreement. 'OK,' he said equably. Something's going on, he thought. There's a mystery, a secret of some sort.

The shoppers got two dinners that day. Rabbit-pie-with-potatoes-and-two-veg at the Ely Guesthouse, and an hour or so later sausage-and-mash at Mrs Murfitt's railway cottage.

Everything was as it should be on a Saturday. Yet Molly still felt as if she were inside her glass jar. A silent and unhappy place, separating her from the rest of the world.

The afternoon was cold, an early winter's day of dazzling light. The sky was so huge and pure that it almost hurt.

As they drew near to Paradise Barn, Molly felt gloomier than ever. She had hoped to be rid of the Pissarro by now. Instead, the painting was still there and it was Cuffey she was rid of.

They'd been trapped by this painting, in its power. They hadn't handed it in because they would be in trouble for keeping it; and the longer they'd kept it the worse trouble they would be in.

When they approached the barn, Adam said, 'The door – it's been shifted! Someone's been here!' He knew immediately that something happened between the two girls in response to what he'd said – something shared and unspoken. He couldn't have said how he knew. A quick glance between them, perhaps, or a slight straightening of shoulders. Or their faces becoming instantly expressionless, to give nothing away. Whatever it was, it excluded him.

One after the other, they slipped inside the half-open door into the shadowy interior.

One of the shadows changed its shape, loomed high and turned to greet them. Rusty Steele, big and tall, with that troubling smile on his face. Adam observed the swagger, the confidence in the man.

'Hi, kids!'

'Hello,' Abigail said guardedly. *Now* what? she thought.

Adam tried to convey a message to them. *Don't look at where the painting is!*

'So this is where you kids like to hang out?' Rusty said.

He stepped towards them and took possession of the space at the centre of the barn. He looked around as if he'd never been there before, surprised, interested. *He's acting,* they thought. *What's he up to?*

'You know,' Rusty said good-humouredly, 'there's something weird about you kids.'

He waited for an answer, got none, and had to carry on without. 'You're always up to something. *Watching* people. D'you know what I call it? I call it *sly!*'

Still no comment from the three 'sly' children.

'I guess you know a lot of things. And you ain't tellin' nobody!'

He prowled for a bit, then sat himself down on an old saw-bench and leaned back against the wall of the building. 'About that flower-press you found,' he said.

There were troubled glances then. They tried to suppress them, but failed.

'Yeah, I heard about that. Now,' he continued slowly, 'it seems to me that there's something strange about that. Why would anyone want to steal a flower-press? A *flower-press*, for Chrissake!'

'Because they like pressing flowers,' Abigail said. There was an edge in her voice that Adam hadn't heard before. But Molly recognised it.

'OK. So why would they *bury* it? In this old place?' Then more loudly, his head pushed forward and down on the last word: 'What's the *point*?'

There was a silence then, all four waiting.

'A flower-press like that – a *big* one – would be useful if you had something that you wanted to keep flat.' Rusty Steele got to his feet and stood in front of them. His voice sank until it was little more than a low growl. 'Like a painting,' he said softly.

'Why don't you leave us alone?' Adam said.

'Because you know what I'm talking about,' Rusty said.

'Gee, mister, we're just little kids having fun,' Abigail said. But Abigail had always been a good mimic and she said this in an almost perfect American drawl. '*Gee, mister, we're jest liddle kids havin' fern.*' Except that it was not quite perfect: it mocked, it was insolent, it was provocative.

It was too much for Rusty Steele. He grabbed Abigail by the hair with his left hand and with his right he gave her a stinging blow across her cheek. She gasped, staggered, and fell against Molly. They both tripped.

It was a good thing Abigail had fallen because Rusty Steele's right hand was already on its way back, for another blow, a back-hander.

Adam lowered his head and rammed himself hard into the man's groin.

'Jesus! You little . . . '

Adam straightened, readying himself for what was coming next. He could see that Molly was hopeless in a fight. All she could think of was Abigail's poor cheek, stark white where it had been struck, quickly flooding scarlet. Abigail was struggling to her feet, her eyes watering. She was gasping for breath.

Rusty Steele was doubled up, clutching himself. But he straightened slowly and clenched both fists. They were big, like loaves of bread.

'Stop right there, Mr Steele! And put your hands up!'

Rusty swung round.

They all stared. Hilda Pritt stood just inside the door, with her revolver in her hand, aimed at the big man's chest.

'Do it!' she snapped. 'Keep them up, high!'

Rusty straightened his body and slowly raised his hands above his head. 'Hilda? Are you some kind of cop?' he said.

Hilda ignored him. 'Are you three OK?' Her voice was icy.

'You aren't . . .' Adam stopped, unable to finish his sentence.

Hilda smiled slightly. She never once took her eyes from Rusty Steele. 'It's all right, Adam,' she said quietly. 'Don't look so disappointed.'

The girls were recovering themselves a little, but Adam was staring at her, reproachful, let down. This was a different Hilda Pritt.

It was strange, the way she spoke directly to Adam while keeping her eyes on Rusty Steele. She seemed to know exactly what was in Adam's mind. 'I *am* in the Air Transport Auxiliary,' she said, 'and I *have* flown all those planes. Everything I told you was true. But there was more to it.'

Hilda turned her attention back to Rusty Steele. 'Back over there!' she snapped in a different tone of voice. 'Stand by that ladder. Now put your hands *on* your head. And keep them there!'

Again, she explained to the children while never taking her eyes off Rusty Steele. 'I've been on a special investigation.'

'What sort of investigation?' Abigail said. Her voice was shaky.

'High level smuggling, Abigail. Between our country and the USA. Not just nylon stockings and cigarettes – important stuff, diamonds, gold bars, spies perhaps. We suspected it was going through the civil flights from near here. My job was to find out.'

'You *bitch*!' Rusty spat out the words.

Hilda raised her eyebrows. 'And because I really *am* an ATA pilot, I was the ideal person to make friends with the American air crews who stayed at the Crown Hotel. I learned a lot that way.'

'Jesus Christ!'

'The stolen Pissarro didn't interest us at first. But the murder of a French art-dealer alerted us. It seemed likely that the stolen painting would find its way here eventually. Or was here already.'

'You can't do me for the killing,' Rusty said.

'No, I can't unfortunately. We know you were in Chicago the night that Mr Dufour was murdered here. And we know who you were with.' Hilda smiled sweetly. 'We've spoken to her,' she said.

Rusty Steele spat.

'And,' Hilda went on, 'no doubt Rusty will spill the beans about who else was in their nasty little plan.'

Molly was totally clear-headed. She saw with perfect clarity, as if they were laid out on a map, how intentions, mistakes, plans and lies were interlinked. She knew instantly that Rusty Steele had a problem. He almost certainly knew, or guessed, that Cuffey had killed the Frenchman. But, if he did know, would he tell? No, she thought – he won't want to admit to any connection with a murder.

Rusty Steele was working this out too; but Molly knew he would say nothing several seconds before he had decided.

'So your alibi for the murder is safe,' Hilda was saying. 'But cheer up! – there's all the other stuff. Not to mention assaulting a child. Oh, yes – I saw that! Are you feeling any better, Abigail?'

Abigail nodded. One absent-minded hand was still rubbing her stinging cheek. But her mind was entirely focused on what was happening. She watched the new Hilda Pritt with admiration and envy. *I want to be like her!* she thought to herself.

'But listen, you three,' Hilda said. 'Mr Steele was right about one thing. Nobody would steal a giant flower-press unless there was something special they wanted to keep flat in it.'

There was a silence. The game was up. There was no point in pretending any more. So Molly went across to the threshing-machine and took out the cardboard tube. She was on the point of explaining that they had planned to take the painting to the police station that afternoon. But she knew it would sound weak, like a feeble excuse for some trivial wrong-doing at school. So she said nothing.

Abigail watched Rusty. She knew exactly what he would do. He glanced at the painting as Molly took it from the cardboard tube, as if he had no interest in it at all, no knowledge of what it might be. Then, while Molly and the painting were the centre of attention, he made a dash for the door of the barn.

But Hilda Pritt had been expecting something like that and she fired her revolver – not at him directly but at the door of the barn, a little ahead of him.

The gunshot stopped him. And the three stood

petrified, staring, their hearing stunned. The entire scene snapped clear in Adam's mind, as if illuminated by a flash of lightning, fixed there in electric black-and-white.

Coolly, with her left hand, Hilda Pritt drew a pair of handcuffs from her shoulder-bag. 'Hold your hands out, Rusty,' she said. 'You can't be trusted to behave.'

The children stared. They'd never seen handcuffs before, except in films. It was a tricky manoeuvre, one which the American might have taken advantage of. He was twice as big as Hilda Pritt. And he was very angry.

'I want one of you,' Hilda said, 'to point the gun at his chest while I slip these on him. It will only take a few seconds.' Her voice was tense.

'Can't *we* put the handcuffs on him?' Adam said.

'No. He would grab you. One of you must hold the revolver.'

Molly would never have fired it. Adam might have got distracted by something. Perhaps Hilda knew that if she wanted single-mindedness it would have to be . . .

'Abigail?'

Abigail took the revolver carefully, balancing its ugly weight, feeling the warmth of Hilda's hand on the grip. She put her index finger on the small metal trigger. She felt very dangerous. She aimed shakily at Rusty's heart and stood well back, out of his reach. But still close enough for an accurate shot. His chest was a big target, hard to miss.

'You two stand away from her line of fire,' Hilda

said. With the handcuffs ready, she approached Rusty from the side.

There was a look of naked terror on Rusty Steele's face as he stared at Abigail. 'Be quick!' he muttered to Hilda Pritt. 'That kid . . . '

The hand that held the gun seemed to have a will of its own – it *wanted* to squeeze the trigger. I would *enjoy* shooting him, Abigail thought. But she didn't have to. Rusty Steele was quickly handcuffed and the gun was back in Hilda's hand.

The interior of the barn suddenly darkened and they realised that a figure had moved into the doorway and shut out the daylight. Sergeant Bly – and another policeman outside, behind him.

The children looked uncertainly at Hilda. 'I arranged back-up,' she said coolly.

About an hour later, Adam pulled the rolled-up painting from its cardboard tube and carefully laid it out flat on the desk at the police-station.

'Pontoise!' Hilda cried. 'How absolutely *lovely*! I've been there ectually. In '36. We had an awfully good time.' The old Hilda had not entirely disappeared.

Rusty Steele had been taken to the back of the building, locked in a cell probably. Sergeant Bly was in the back room, telephoning a senior policeman at Ely.

'Will we be in trouble?' Molly whispered.

'Trouble?' Hilda said. 'I don't see why you should

be in trouble. You deserve medals! All three of you!'

Was it to be as simple as that? It didn't seem quite right somehow. Molly badly wanted to cry. She turned her face onto Abigail's shoulder.

Something puzzled Adam. 'Why did Mr Steele come back to the Barn today?'

'*Back* to it?'

'Yes. He had already searched it – some days ago.'

'How do you know that?'

'We saw him,' Abigail said through Molly's hair. 'We watch everybody.'

'I think I know why he came back,' Hilda said. 'I'd heard about how you had found the missing flower-press, but I thought at first it was just an ordinary one. When I found out how big it was, I realised why it had been stolen. But it was just a village story, a bit of local gossip that the American airmen wouldn't even hear about. So, today, when we were all having breakfast, I just happened to mention it. And I stressed the fact that it was a *very big* flower-press. And that it was you three who had found it – in the barn.'

Just happened to mention it! Adam thought. She went on about it for twenty minutes!

'Did you suspect him?'

'Yes. And I thought: if he is involved, he will go to the barn and search it.'

'And he did,' Abigail said with satisfaction.

'I didn't know you three were going there too,' Hilda said. 'Sorry!'

But Molly still wasn't happy. 'What about the murder?' she said.

At that moment, Sergeant Bly came back into the office and sat down at his desk, facing them.

'The murder? Well, that's not my job, actually,' Hilda said. 'That's a police matter. We've been working together, of course,' – here she glanced at the Sergeant – 'and I'll give them all my information. But my job's done – well, it will be when I've written my report.'

Where is Cuffey now, at this minute? Molly wondered sadly. 'Will they catch the murderer?' she said.

'Probably. They usually do, you know,' Hilda said.

'Though in wartime it's different,' Sergeant Bly admitted. 'People seem able to disappear more easily.'

Very slowly, the mood was lightening, as if sunshine were finally breaking through an endless fog.

'Cheer up, do!' Hilda said. 'You are heroes! Absolute heroes! First you find a missing flower-press, which makes an old lady very happy. Then you capture an enemy pilot. That ought to be enough for anyone! But then you go and retrieve a priceless stolen painting!'

And Charlie Leggett's broken shovel, Molly thought, though she knew there was not much glory in that. 'But the murder?' she said.

'Ah,' said Hilda Pritt, 'you'd be *super*heroes if you had also found out who did that!'

'Now,' the sergeant said, 'I think we've done. You can all go – and later I'll pay a visit to your mums. They'll be really proud of you, I shouldn't wonder.'

He turned to Adam. 'And if you give me your address, young man, I'll write to your parents.'

'I haven't got an address,' Adam said. 'We haven't got a house any more.'

There was no bitterness in his voice, no anger. He was just stating the facts. 'But I can give you addresses for my mum and dad,' he said.

They had spent a long afternoon at the police station. Outside, it was cold and almost dark.

'What about tea and cakes in Auntie Marge's?' Hilda said. 'You deserve a treat.'

Auntie Marge's tea-room was not as smart as it had been before the War, partly because the government had said that it was illegal to sell iced cakes. But Auntie Marge still served tea and coffee, with biscuits and a small range of buns. Abigail and Molly had been there a few times, but Adam never had.

So in they went, ordering drinks and slices of sponge-cake. There were mischievous rumours in the town about how Auntie Marge managed to keep making such wonderful cakes, what with the War and food shortages. It was said that she put soot in her chocolate sponges. But Hilda cared nothing for such doubts.

Adam had begun to forgive Hilda for not being exactly what she'd seemed. Still, there were many things he didn't understand. Perhaps Hilda knew that –

because, when she started explaining, it was Adam she mostly looked at.

'Ready?' she asked. 'Paying attention?'

They were all ears, even Molly.

'Before the War I worked for Special Investigations,' Hilda said. 'Secret stuff. But when the War broke out I left and joined the ATA. I had done some flying in peace-time and I thought I could be useful. I had a jolly good time and made a lot of flights. I told you about some of them, Adam. But then I was called back for a special job.'

'The smuggling?' Abigail said.

'Quite right, Abigail. High level smuggling. Between our country and the USA. We suspected it was going through the civil flights from near here. Special Investigations wanted me to find out.'

Auntie Marge brought a tea-tray. She was all ears and took a long time laying out the things.

'When you're on a job, you have to have what we call a *cover*. Often it's a pretence and you have to learn it up. It's jolly hard work! But my cover had a big advantage – it was true. I really *was* an ATA pilot. That's why I was chosen for the job. It was easy to make friends with the American air crews who stayed at the Crown Hotel. And I learned a lot. But *you* thought I was a bally idiot, didn't you?'

'Adam didn't,' Abigail said.

'Anyway, the stolen Pissarro was nothing to do with it at first. There was nothing to connect it with the contraband that was getting through from here. But the murder of the French art-dealer changed all that. His body had been found within a mile of the Crown Hotel we were investigating. So we were sure there was a link – it couldn't just be a coincidence. It seemed likely that the stolen painting would find its way here eventually.'

There was a touch of the miraculous about Hilda that afternoon. Abigail and Adam were both falling a little in love with her. Adam was deeply happy that she was – after all – everything he had hoped she was. Abigail gazed at her in a rapture, determined to be an ATA pilot when she grew up. Molly was more resistant. She was uneasy with people who could slip in and out of disguises.

'For a while, we suspected Cuffey. I'm sorry, Molly, but I had a job to do. Anyway, I checked and he really *was* working for the War Department, as he said. Surveying bridges or something. So we took him off the list of suspects.'

Molly felt her face going red.

'Do you miss him, Molly?' Hilda said.

Molly looked up, surprised at Hilda's gentleness. She nodded. There's no point in pretending, she thought.

'He left very suddenly. Did you know he was planning to go away?'

Abigail fell silent and still. She watched Molly carefully.

'No,' Molly said. 'Not until just before he went.'

'Was that why he took you out for a walk – yesterday, after school?' Adam said.

'A walk?' Hilda said. 'But it must have been almost dark! And it was raining kets-n-dawgs!'

'We often went for walks,' Molly said.

'I know you did, sweetie! But why *then*?'

'He knew I wouldn't want him to go away. He wanted to tell me himself.'

Hilda attentive. Abigail watchful. Adam puzzled.

'Where did you go?'

This is the moment, Abigail thought. This is the tipping point. If Molly tells Hilda that they'd walked in the dark across muddy fields to the barn, that will lead to the truth, a confession. Abigail suddenly knew she didn't want that. Molly had promised herself that she would not give Cuffey away; and Abigail – the believer in justice and punishment – didn't want Molly to break her promise to herself.

'They went to the river,' she said. 'To the bridge. He liked going there.'

Now Molly will never tell. And nor can I, Abigail thought. Ever!

'I saw them,' she added. 'When they crossed the railway.' (The first part of that, at least, was true.)

Hilda Pritt possessed amazing aeronautical skills – but she hadn't the slightest idea of the emotional currents passing between two people only inches away from her. 'Did he tell you when he's coming back?' she asked cheerfully.

'I don't think he's coming back at all.'

Hilda smiled kindly at Molly's long face. 'So it really was a proper goodbye?' she said.

A *proper* goodbye? Molly's lie was in danger of being overlaid by the truth – the shifty and hang-dog way Cuffey had finally left the barn. 'Not really,' she said sadly.

Oh, those big eyes! Abigail thought. They will give us away if she's not careful.

Hilda hesitated. Then she put her hand on Molly's and said, 'That was a bit shabby of him. You rather liked him, didn't you? The least he could have done was say goodbye properly.' Hilda was interested by Molly's story, but not suspicious. 'But you mustn't be too severe on him, Molly,' she said. 'My granny used to say you should never judge people by their worst actions.'

Then Molly began to warm towards Hilda, a little. It might have been because they had got through those tricky questions about Cuffey's goodbye. But it was also because of what Hilda had said. *You should never judge people by their worst actions.* She thought that was rather wise. I'll write it down when I get home, she thought. She memorised it. *You should never judge people . . .*

Yet it still wasn't enough. It helped, but it wasn't enough. It didn't explain what had happened in the barn with Cuffey.

Abigail turned the conversation in a different direction. 'How *is* your granny?' she said. 'Did she get bombed?'

Hilda was startled. 'What do you know about my granny?' she demanded.

'We followed you to Little Green one Saturday.'

Hilda gaped.

'We thought you were a spy, watching the airfield.'

'Then you found out that I was just visiting my dear old grandmother!'

Abigail nodded happily.

'Well, I must say, you three take the jolly biscuit! And my grandmother is fine, thankyou very much. She's gone to stay with my parents until the bombing eases off.'

Adam had a question for Hilda. 'Why didn't you come and help with the German pilot that day? Was it really just because you wanted to have a bath?'

'Well, *really*! You didn't expect me to *believe* that story, did you? I thought it was some game, or a trick or something. Like those demned silly questions you'd asked me! *How many bombs can a Spitfire carry? I ask you!*'

She has a nice smile, Molly thought.

Demned silly, Abigail said inside her head. *Demned silly*. She wanted to be able to say it the way Hilda did. But she knew her mum wouldn't allow her to say it at all.

'I only realised that it was true when I came out of the bathroom and saw that you'd taken the Webley from my bag! Bloomin' cheek, if you don't mind my saying so.'

Hilda had changed everything. She was the Hilda Pritt they had wanted her to be. Breezy and brave, bringing sunshine and optimism.

Under the table, Molly felt for Abigail's hand. Molly felt a lot better – almost happy!

Three weeks later, they received an unexpected visit.

They had been questioned by the police – more than once – and they'd had to make statements. Press reporters had arrived too. And they were questioned again, later, when three art experts drove down from London to examine the Pissarro. They were taken out of school for that, which made it more interesting.

A great fuss was made about the damage that the painting might have suffered. One of the experts was deeply distressed when he heard that it had spent time under a mattress in a damp caravan. And when he learned that it had been rolled up and left in a barn, he turned pale and had to be helped to the nearest chair.

For goodness' sake, Molly thought. It's only a picture! If it's badly damaged, get someone to paint another one!

Abigail and Adam tried to make Molly understand about great art. But she just sniffed and said it was silly nonsense.

All the national daily papers carried short news items about the discovery, without naming the children.

But the local weekly newspaper did them proud. The *Deeping and Ely Gazette* had pictures of them on the front page and the whole story told in full. The headline was: *LOCAL YOUNG HEROES DO THEIR BIT*.

'We're famous!' Abigail kept saying. 'We're famous.' But she still got told off at school when her sums were wrong, and she still had to help her mum do the same jobs at home. What was the point of being famous, she thought, if it made no difference?

Molly wondered why no-one minded that they had kept the painting so long. She suspected that Mrs Weathergreen was responsible. She too had been interviewed because of her flower-press. No untruths were told – Molly was sure of that – but somehow the impression was given that the children had patiently cared for the painting until they discovered how valuable it was, and that a thief was trying to find it.

She was thankful, of course. But it made her wonder if the truth was ever exactly told.

People said to them: 'You'll get a reward. Finding an important painting like that! Bound to!'

But there was no reward, at least not officially.

But one day after school, when all three of the children were in the kitchen with Molly's mum, Mrs Weathergreen and Mr Morton came to call.

Mrs Weathergreen was a familiar visitor. But Mr Morton wasn't – a tall, serious, rather daunting person. A man of few words. They were welcomed, settled on chairs and given cups of tea. And all the time Molly's mum kept looking at Molly with an expression which meant: Why are *they* here? What have you done *now*?

Mrs Weathergreen wasted no time. 'We think these children should be rewarded for what they did,' she said. 'They were honest and brave and true-hearted.'

We weren't exactly *honest*, Abigail thought.

I didn't feel brave, Molly thought.

What's Mr Morton got to do with it? Adam wondered.

'Mr Morton and I are old friends. So I talked it over with him.'

Mrs Barnes knew that Mr Morton had twice asked Mrs Weathergreen to marry him – once when she was not much more than a girl and again, later, when she was a widow.

'You tell them, Charles,' Mrs Weathergreen said.

Mr Morton turned towards the three. 'You're to play in the barn,' he said. 'Whenever you want.' His words were slow and measured. He spoke in exactly the same way he might have spoken to one of his labourers – 'I want Black Fen Field ploughed.' He turned to Mrs Barnes, and said with great emphasis, as if she might not have understood, '*Whenever they want!*'

Play in it? Molly thought. We've been playing in it for years! What sort of reward is it if you get given something you already have? It was an unworthy thought, and she was ashamed of it. But still . . .

Adam's thoughts were different. It had never

occurred to him that the barn belonged to anyone. He had thought that it was just there – like the river, or the level-crossing, or London Bridge.

Mr Morton saw that Molly's mum was puzzled and about to say something. He spoke quickly, to forestall her. 'I only use it for rubbish,' he said. 'Old machinery that I'm never going to use.'

'But, Mr Morton . . . '

'What?' he demanded. He was a difficult man to say no to (though Mrs Weathergreen had done it twice).

'I don't really like them being there at all,' she said. 'After what has happened. *And* they've been caught there in an air-raid.'

'Just as safe under one of my farm machines as in your shelter,' the farmer said.

'It's not very . . .' Mrs Barnes hesitated, searching for the right word. 'It's not very *cosy*.'

Oh, *Mum!* Molly thought.

'Oh, but it *is*!' said Mrs Weathergreen. Eyes wide open, and voice a little hushed as if she were telling a story to the smallest children in the Sunday School, she said, 'You don't know about the hay-room. *That's* what Mr Morton particularly wants the children to use. The *hay-room*.'

The children became more interested. What hay-room?

'I'll move the rubbish this weekend,' Mr Morton said.

'It's quite big – almost as big as this kitchen,' Mrs Weathergreen said.

'Put a pane of glass in the window. No trouble.'

'It's got a small fireplace,' Mrs Weathergreen added.

'A fireplace?'

'Stable-lads slept there,' Mr Morton said. 'In history. My great-grandfather's time.'

'We've never seen it,' Abigail said doubtfully.

'Sheets of corrugated iron,' Mr Morton said. In his language, this meant that the hay-room was hidden behind the rusty sheets of corrugated iron stacked up against it.

'Has it got a brick floor, like the rest of the barn?' Molly asked.

'Oh, no, dear! A wooden floor. It's upstairs.'

Upstairs! It was growing better with every word.

Molly's mum brightened a little. 'It does sound rather nice,' she said. It was the first time for weeks that she had smiled like that – and a quick understanding flashed through Molly's mind that the War had made her mother tired and worried.

'You go up a wooden staircase. There's no stair-rail, so you'd have to be careful. But it's perfectly safe. There's a small platform at the top, and a door.

'Like a signal-box,' Abigail said.

Mr Morton nodded. 'Except for three hundred years,' he said. He was talking about history again.

The two visitors left soon after that. 'A week,' Mr Morton said. 'I'll have it cleared in a week.'

It was a good reward, Molly thought afterwards. It turned their excitement towards the future instead of the past. They began to make plans about finding an old table, and some chairs, and some coal for the fireplace. Abigail said the room would need a rug.

The possibilities were endless.

Wednesday 11th December ~ evening

On Wednesday afternoon, they were walking slowly home from school. The three of them, in the gathering frosty darkness.

As they crossed the top of Marquis Way, Molly noticed a soldier walking slowly towards the town. This was a common sight. He walked as if he was tired. He wore a greatcoat and various bulky army packs, and he carried his rifle and his kitbag.

They crossed the top of the road. Molly was looking forward to getting indoors and settling down for the evening. Abigail would come round later, scurrying through the dark.

'Molly!' Abigail said. She spoke in an urgent whisper.

Molly turned.

'That soldier! It's your Dad!'

Molly's heart leapt painfully in her body. 'It isn't,' she said. But her voice was uncertain.

She looked again. The soldier was behind them now and it was hard for them to look back without seeming rude. It couldn't be, could it?

Molly took in the pale face, the tiredness in his

movements, and – he was *smaller* than she remembered, dwarfed by the uniform. Even his face was sharper under its lop-sided khaki hat.

It *was* him, though. She knew now. How could she have passed by her own father, and failed to recognise him? What would he be thinking of his daughter, that she could do such a thing? She began to run towards him and she saw him drop his kitbag to the ground, quickly put down his rifle and straighten up with his arms out to contain her. There was a blissful passionate hug. Molly pressed her soft cheeks against her Dad's rough face.

'Is that Abigail?' he asked quietly into her ear.

Then Molly's heart was smitten with guilt. She spoke quietly in the private centre of their hug. 'Abigail's Dad is . . . '

'Oh, *no!* He hasn't been . . . ?'

'Missing, feared killed,' Molly said.

'Micky? Old Micky Murfitt? He and I used to . . . '

Molly was stricken with concern for Abigail. Then, in a burst of generosity and idealism, she suddenly knew that she would let Abigail share *her* father. He could be her father too, and everything would be all right. All she had to do was explain to Abigail how it would be.

But that idea was dismissed before it came fully into being. It was foolish, she knew. It would be meaningless to tell Abigail they could share the same father.

Mr Barnes had turned to Abigail and was speaking

246

to her. And Abigail was doing the business, being polite. She was telling him all about the evacuee boy and introducing him. 'This is Adam,' she said. 'He's living at your house. He's OK, but he does daft things. But you should see him draw!'

'How long are you home for, Mr Barnes?'

'Till after Christmas. I've got embarkation leave.'

'Embrocation leave?' Abigail said. 'Have you got a bad back?'

'Em*bark*ation, Abigail. It means this is a special leave because I'm going overseas.'

'Whereabouts overseas?' Molly said, suddenly anxious.

'Well, we're not supposed to know. But everyone says it'll be North Africa.'

Abigail watched as Molly and her Dad, along with Adam, went into the Ely Guesthouse. Molly was flushed and her eyes had darkened. Abigail knew that look. She turned back once and saw that Molly's Mum had come out into the road and was hugging Mr Barnes. Adam had gone inside and Abigail, in her mind's eye, could see him in the big kitchen, already opening his sketch-book or sharpening a pencil.

Comics for me tonight, Abigail thought.

She walked slowly homewards, quietly kicking a stone along with her as she went. When she got there she climbed onto one of the railway gates. Her Mum had closed them to traffic, ready for a goods train on the down line from London.

Abigail climbed onto the big railway gate, rested her arms along the top and decided to watch the train go through. She would count the trucks. The train approached through the darkness. The thump and hiss of the black locomotive shook the road as it passed, and the driver gave her an unhurried regal wave. Then came the rhythmic clatter of the trucks, on and on.

Abigail was not gloomy for long. Across the darkening fen, she could see in the distance the black bulk of Paradise Barn silhouetted against the last light of the south-western sky. That lifted her spirits. They were going to make a start there on Saturday.

But it wasn't over yet, this story.

On the evening after school had broken up for Christmas the three of them settled at Abigail's house. The girls were sharing the sofa, crouching together with the latest issue of *Beano*. Adam sat at the table, working at a charcoal drawing.

It was a picture of Cuffey, seated on a chair in Molly's dining-room.

Abigail's mum could be heard moving about in the kitchen. Every now and again, she called out sharp little reminders about good behaviour: 'Don't you dare make marks on my table-cloth with those mucky chalks!' or 'If you keep swinging back on that chair, Adam Swales, you'll make great holes in the lino!'

Adam liked it. He found it comforting.

The railway bell clanged and they heard the back door slam shut as Mrs Murfitt went out to the crossing-gates.

'I wonder *why* he left,' Abigail said. They had been talking about Cuffey.

Adam's drawing-hand took a rest for a moment, while he paid attention. What were they up to, those girls? There was something behind the question – a touch of mischief.

But Adam had some mischief of his own. 'I expect it was because he knew they were closing in on him,' he said.

Both girls were instantly alert. They stared at him, on their guard. He rather liked it.

'Who was closing in?'

'The police,' Adam said nonchalantly.

'*Why?*'

'Because he was the murderer.'

He had startled them, that was clear. But not quite in the way he'd expected. Had they worked it out for themselves?

'What makes you so sure of that?' Abigail demanded.

Adam considered a moment. 'I didn't say I was *sure.*'

'Well, then!' Abigail said, as if that settled it.

Why was Abigail so cross? 'But I bet he was, all the same,' he added.

Molly remained silent. It was Abigail who demanded to know if he had any evidence. The question was dismissive – she knew he couldn't have.

Adam pointed a charcoally finger. 'The right-hand pocket of his jacket,' he said.

Abigail and Molly left the sofa and crowded over Adam's drawing. They studied the pocket, lumpy, pulling the side of the jacket out of shape.

'It was hard to get it right,' Adam said.

'So what?'

'It's like life-drawing. If an artist wants to draw people's bodies, he has to understand what's inside. Bones. And muscles.'

They took this in, worked it out, and understood. 'Well?'

'I couldn't get the pocket right until I knew what was in it. I thought at first that he kept a pipe and a tin of tobacco there.'

'He didn't smoke,' Molly said.

'No. It wasn't a pipe.'

'You didn't *look*?' Abigail, shocked and disapproving. But deeply interested all the same.

Adam nodded. It hadn't occurred to him that he shouldn't. 'That last afternoon. He was upstairs, talking to Molly. He'd left his jacket hanging on the chair.'

Adam watched them – two girls' faces, pale in the gas-light, big eyes, darkly shadowed.

'It was a gun.'

He saw them look at each other briefly. Was it fear?

'A gun?'

'Like Hilda's?'

'Not exactly like Hilda's. I didn't have time to see what kind it was – but it wasn't the same as hers.'

'Was it loaded?' Molly whispered.

'I think so. Then I heard him coming downstairs with you. So I had to put it back.'

The gas-mantles hissed softly in Mrs Murfitt's living-room. A burning coal slipped slightly and some ash gently cascaded from the grate.

'Why didn't you tell anyone?' Abigail asked.

To Molly, this conversation seemed to move incredibly slowly. There were acres of dusky silence between each thing said.

Adam shrugged. 'It's not against the law to have a gun. Hilda Pritt had one.'

A small coal exploded softly on the fire. Outside, the crossing-gates crashed back into place.

'Then he came down with Molly, grabbed his jacket and coat, and went out. Where were you *really* going?'

'We went for a walk,' Molly said. 'You know that.' Every bit of her was alert, in protection of Cuffey, and what she had done.

'Why didn't you tell us?' Abigail demanded.

'I *am* telling you,' Adam said.

They heard Mrs Murfitt coming back into the kitchen. The back door was shut, a lid banged onto a saucepan.

'He might have shot Molly!'

Adam looked at Abigail as if she was mad. 'Don't be daft,' he said. 'He wouldn't hurt Molly.'

'How can you be so sure?'

Adam pointed again at his drawing. They had already seen the rapt look on Cuffey's face. But when the girls studied it more closely, they saw there was another presence, deep in the shadows. It was Molly, crouched on the floor, looking down, reading a book perhaps. She was viewed from behind, hardly there at all. Yet she *was* there – and it was Molly that Cuffey was looking at with such affection.

Abigail and Adam went on talking about the gun in Cuffey's pocket. Abigail couldn't leave the subject alone. 'So he definitely had his gun in his pocket when he went out with Molly?' she said.

'Yes.' Why was Abigail making such a fuss about it?

Molly, kneeling on the floor, gazed at the flickering fire. Understanding was penetrating her mind as rain soaks into the ground. There was a horrible sick fear at first; then a slow realisation; finally, a deep and tearful thankfulness. She knew then what had kept her safe in the barn that night – kept them both safe, in fact.

She turned and saw the other two, unsure, and irritated with each other. Abigail looked at her across the room. The expression on her face said *Shall I tell him?*

Molly nodded. She wanted to be done with all these secrets. And she didn't like Adam being left out.

The telling was long and delicious, with puzzled questions and quick whispered answers. Abigail did all of it at first, then Molly joined in.

In this story, I have made a few changes to history.

In January 1940, there were eight women pilots in the Air Transport Auxiliary; Hilda Pritt was the (fictional) ninth. And I have taken some liberties with their flying schedules. They were not allowed to fly combat-planes until later in the War; and it is very unlikely that Hilda would have flown fighters to and from France. But what she says about Amy Johnson is true: the famous aviator did fly for the ATA. She died serving in it in January 1941, when her plane crashed into the Thames estuary.

The Morrison Shelter – the table-shelter which Molly has to crawl into during air-raids – was widely used during the War, but it was not in fact available until 1941.

There were many air-bases in East Anglia, but the American B24 Liberator, which was flying between Britain and the United States during this period, is more likely to have flown to and from Lyneham or Northolt.

By September 1940, Germany had invaded and overrun most of continental Europe, and driven the defeated British Army from Dunkirk. An invasion was expected at any time, especially during the weekend beginning on Friday 6th September. Chiefs of staff had agreed that the codeword *Cromwell* was to be used to indicate that a German invasion was taking place. Church bells were to be rung as a call to arms. However, there was a good deal of confusion and in the evening of September 7th church bells in many towns – especially in East Anglia – were rung by mistake.

The German landing, Operation *Sealion*, never happened. Instead, a massive series of bombing-raids began on British towns and cities. The blitz had begun.

Great Deeping is a fictional town. I have placed it and its surrounding countryside a few miles north of Littleport and a few miles south of Downham Market. To achieve this, I have added several miles to the length of the River Great Ouse and the railway from London to King's Lynn.

The artist Camille Pissarro painted many views of Pontoise in France, but the painting described in this story is fictional.

In old currency, there were 240 pence in a pound, 12 pence in a shilling, and 20 shillings in a pound. A shilling was the equivalent of 5p in today's money. And school half-term holidays rarely lasted a full week.